HER AMETHYST PENDANT

A GUARDIANS OF CAMELOT PORTAL FANTASY NOVEL

SARAH BIGLOW

For information contact; www.sarah-biglow.com

Edited by: Alecia Goodman, Under Wraps Publishing Services

Cover Design by: Deranged Doctor Design

Interior Art by: Therena Carlin

Print ISBN: 978-1-955988-41-4

10 9 8 7 6 5 4 3 2 1

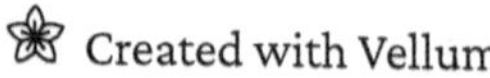 Created with Vellum

FROM THE AUTHOR

Special Thanks to:

Victoria Psomiadis, Ryan Scott James, Brian Grimes, Anonymous Reader, maileguy, Rosie Pease, Samantha Newberry, Tanya Young, Heiko Koenig, Yara Dijkstra, Samantha Ghormley, GhostCat, pjk, Jackie Kripas, Elizabeth W., Ayl, Matthew Walker, Chris Clayton, Francesco Tehrani, Stacy Ward, Catherine McP., Mono, Emily Welsby, Sue Frecker, Diane Hansebout, Lavar, Anna McCluskey, Vicki Hsu, Molly Zenk, Lorenzo, Michael W. Kerr, Scott Casey, Kathryn, Bonniejean Boettecher, Katherine Malloy, Melissa Showers, Gerald P. McDaniel, Finley Ymir, Niels Starfari, Stephen Ballentine, StarbuckApolloFemshepKaidanAliCole,, Danae, Susanna, PippiMD, Isaac Dansicker, Steven Byrd, Robin Hill, John Idlor, Nicola Thompson, Stacy Shuda, Adam Brooks, Courtney Arnold, Margaret St. John, Molly J. Stanton, Cathy McLoughlin, Billye Herndon, Justise Briones, Amanda, Alexandra Corrsin, Maria Mejia, Josefine Bällsten, Vanessa Goodwin, Jade Feinics, and Karen Bulgarelli.

ONE

Early morning sunlight glittered off the lake's surface as I sat on the bank, my gaze searching for signs of my companion. For nearly three months we'd been meeting like this, sharing the quiet stillness and getting to know one another. Finally, a large shadow blotted out the light as Taron descended from the clouds, landing softly on the grass beside me. I watched as the scales and bulk of his dragon form melted back into dark skin and toned muscle, until the man I'd first met in this very spot stood before me.

His casual comfort with nudity still amazed me. At least I'd gotten used to it to the point where I didn't gawk at him with embarrassment warming my cheeks.

"You're late," I noted.

He offered a mock bow and flashed a broad smile. "My deepest apologies, Your Highness. Please allow me to make it up to you."

"Oh, sod off," I replied with a laugh.

He approached the water's edge and gestured to the unbroken surface. "You still owe me that swim."

"I haven't forgotten. But it's got to be freezing."

He waded waist deep before turning around in challenge. "It feels fine to me."

"Says the man who can literally make water evaporate on command," I muttered.

He took a step closer, extending a hand for me to take. "Come on, I promise you won't freeze."

I couldn't deny a part of me wanted to dive in just to be close to him. Even after all of these stolen mornings together, it wasn't like we were in a place where that sort of intimacy was on the table. He fixed me with a pleading look that tugged at more than just my heart.

Damn it.

"Fine." I kicked off my shoes and socks, and stood, undoing the button and zipper on my pants. "But you aren't getting all of this." I gestured to the rest of my body.

The pleading look turned serious. "I would never

ask you to do something that made you uncomfortable."

Fuck, why did he have to be so chivalrous?

With that, I shimmied out of my jeans and pulled my shirt over my head. I stood there in my bra and underwear shivering in the brisk November air. From the water, Taron's hands began to glow a pale yellow. He lowered them into the water, and I watched as the surface broke with bubbles and wisps of steam drifted into the air.

"Come on in," he called.

When I didn't immediately rush into the water, he splashed me. Warm water—the temperature I would expect from a bath—hit my bare legs. He smirked as he prepared for another volley. Only I didn't give him the chance this time. I marched in, feeling my toes dig into the soft lakebed beneath us. I made it into the water up to my hips before he lunged forward and wrapped his arms around my waist. Tiny water droplets clung to his eyelashes, making his brown irises sparkle even more.

"You really are unlike any man I've ever met," I whispered.

"I will take that for the compliment I hope it to be," he said.

I fell silent as I took in his appearance up close. I

longed to trace the sharpness of his jaw line with my finger or heaven help me kiss him.

Are dragons this realm's sex magnets?

"You went away for a moment. Where did you go?" His voice pulled me back to reality.

"Sorry, just wondering ... are all dragons so attractive?"

"You think I'm attractive?"

"Oh, please. Have you looked in a mirror? I mean, are you all this damned hot or is it just a you thing?" The words fell out of my mouth before I could stop them.

"You've met other dragons. What do you think?"

Definitely a him thing.

"Uh, I think that you don't have a right to be this gorgeous. How is it no one's already come along and laid claim to you?"

"You make it sound like I am a piece of property to be owned. I would have thought such archaic things beneath you."

"I just meant you're a prince and objectively gorgeous. Are all the women in your kingdom blind?"

"Well, there have been suitors, but none have interested me. They lacked the ability to hide their true intentions."

"And what were those intentions?"

"A crown."

"So, you stepping down must have pissed off a lot of people then."

"Only those who believed I should not have the right to step aside and let my sister rule when the time comes."

"You really just don't want to be king?"

"Some of us are born to lead nations. And some of us are born to craft beautiful things in other ways."

His right hand moved from my waist to my wrist. He kicked his feet, pulling me toward the center of the lake. "I would think you of all people would understand the desire to be something other than the role you were born into."

"I mean, I never really believed I'd be in line for a throne. But I never thought I'd spend my days slinging drinks either." After a moment, I added. "I guess sometimes I'm a little jealous of your freedom."

"Well, do not be too jealous. Just because I am no longer destined for a throne doesn't mean I do not have duties that weigh on me."

"I also can't believe no one notices you sneaking off every morning."

"I could say the same for you," he retorted, the water rippling around as he kept us both afloat with an effortless grace. It made me wonder if he secretly possessed aquatic powers, too.

I'd never been an early riser back in London, mostly because of all the late nights working at the bar. But since coming to Camelot, I'd found a reason to wake before sunrise. Plus, it had given me a chance to practice my portal magic. Emerys should be proud that I'd honed this particular skill. Jumping from one place to another was bound to come in handy one of these days.

"Morgan?" His voice drew me out of my head again.

"Sorry," I murmured. "I don't think they're used to me being around the castle full-time. I mean, I showed up, stayed what ... a week and then flitted off on a quest? My mother keeps joking we ought to have some sort of meet and greet with all the staff, so they know who I am."

"Your subjects should get to know you, especially given what transpired with Arthur."

I bristled at the mention of Arthur's name. He'd been absent from my thoughts for months and I was content for it to stay that way. On some level, I knew I couldn't wholly blame him for taking the life that had been meant for me. Yet, I hated him for it, especially the way he had flaunted his position and power when we first met. The cockiness and swagger made him perennially punchable in my book.

"I think that's what Emerys worries about with doing such a public gathering. She thinks there are still people loyal to him within the ranks."

"She is a wise woman," he said. "I do not envy your mother the task of rooting out loyalists."

"I think she's still trying to keep me out of all the court stuff. Like maybe if I'm distanced from all the bureaucracy then it will be easier to protect me."

"Well, I would argue you are perfectly capable of protecting yourself." He flashed me a flirtatious grin. "Especially with what we've been practicing."

Heat danced down my spine at his words. We hadn't just been coming here to chat. I knew that whatever else lay ahead of me, this world operated on combat. And a bartender from London who knew how to sling drinks, and not weapons needed to train.

"Yeah, well, I still feel like I've got a lot to learn."

"Should we practice then?" he offered, kicking with powerful momentum towards shore.

My body protested the change in venue. But my

brain knew that getting in some sword practice was a more appropriate use of our time. Especially if anyone happened to spy on us. We didn't need some errant courier spreading rumors.

"Only if you do that whole evaporating-water trick on my clothes, too. I'm not taking a portal home soaking wet. I'd freeze."

"Then perhaps you should have brought a towel," he quipped as he eased me out of the water. With my feet firmly back on solid grassy ground, I gave him a playful glare as the dampness vanished from his skin. I arched a brow at him as he tugged on his pants.

"I'm waiting."

"Milady," he said in an exaggerated bow. With a flourish he rubbed his hands together as if mimicking starting a fire and a wave of heat rippled forth from his outstretched fingers. In a matter of moments my bra and underwear were dry.

"Thank you."

"Get dressed. As you said, we've got work to do."

I staggered into my jeans and tugged my shirt over my head as he produced a blade from under his shirt.

I pressed my left index finger to the tiny

sapphire on the bracelet around my right wrist. The silver metal of the jewelry sparkled in the morning light. With a rush that I still hadn't gotten used to after all these months, the bracelet morphed. The form changing until it became an elegant sword with a large sapphire in its hilt.

Excalibur.

I settled my weight back on my heels and raised the sword. With an elegant movement, Taron advanced on me. I lifted the blade to block his attack and metal clanged against metal. The way he pressed forward forced me to lose a few steps as I fought to just parry his swings.

"You're doing it again," he chided.

"Doing what?" I barely dodged a side swipe directed toward my ribs.

"Getting distracted."

He wasn't wrong. From the start of our little training sessions, I'd found it hard to concentrate fully on the task at hand. The fluidity of his movements was like watching a professional display their craft. It was beautiful. He was made to wield a sword.

"Well, I'm sorry but you are very distracting," I replied.

"I could blindfold you," he offered and feinted left.

I switched my grip on Excalibur's pommel, bringing it down to deflect just in time to avoid him slicing into my thigh. "Only if you want everything to end up in tatters."

He stopped his advances and settled the sword at his side. The jovial expression he'd worn a moment ago was gone, replaced by a stern look. "It is not a joke. It would allow you to hone and rely on your other senses. Because the enemies we face are not always what they appear to be."

Another shiver danced down my spine as I recalled the way in which the Seelies change their appearance. Sure, dragons could too, but somehow that felt less terrifying. Maybe all of the time I'd been spending around Taron had tempered that fear.

"Okay, you are probably right ... it would help. But I don't like not being able to see what I'm doing."

He took a step closer. "I know, but that is the whole point. You have to be ready to defend yourself in any situation." He tapped the flat of his sword against Excalibur. "Now, I'm not going to ruin a perfectly good shirt, so close your eyes."

I wanted to protest, but I couldn't deny his reasoning. I gave a soft huff anyway and raised Excalibur into a fighting stance and shut my eyes. "I'm ready."

Nothing happened at first other than I felt panic rising in my chest at the realization I didn't know what was going on around me. It burned like acid in my throat and my hands turned clammy as nausea took over.

You can do this Morgan.

The words sounded in my head, but the voice sounded eerily like Aunt Nim. I took comfort in the thought she was still watching over me and guiding me. Exhaling to calm the anxiety, I tried to focus on what I could hear, smell, and feel.

My ears picked up on the sound of grass crunching beneath Taron's feet. It was subtle but there, moving around my righthand side. I gripped Excalibur's pommel in both hands and prepared to swing to my right. I let out a grunt as my blade sliced through empty air.

"You were close," Taron encouraged, his voice floated from my left now.

I pivoted a little to face where it sounded like he was coming from. Though maybe my hearing wasn't the best thing to rely on. I tried to take a deep breath, letting his scent fill my nose. In that moment I realized he always seemed to smell a bit of musk and ash. It was in the air all around me—probably because he had the same scent in both dragon and human form—but it was stronger when I turned my head to the left. I felt the ground shift beneath my feet and brought the blade up.

Metal struck metal and I opened my eyes.

Somehow, I'd managed to block his attack and he was grinning at me. "Good!"

"It felt like luck," I said.

"For your first try, it was wonderful. We'll keep practicing and tomorrow I will actually bring a blindfold."

"You really don't have to sound so excited about depriving me of my sight," I quipped.

"I think we've done enough for now," he said, readying to stow his sword.

I'd spent the morning on the offensive. Time to try a little defense. I lunged forward and Taron barely brought the sword up to meet my attack.

"I said we were done." His tone turned sharp, and orange flared around his irises.

"Shit! I didn't mean to piss you off," I said, taking a step back and allowing Excalibur to fall to my side.

His face softened a little. "I am happy to train with you Morgan, but you forget, the blade you wield has power. It can do real damage, even if you don't intend it."

I looked down at the sword in my hand. The sapphire in the hilt glinted in the morning sunlight and I shivered. I'd felt the sword's power before. At times, it felt as though the weapon had a sentience and guided me when I felt lost. He was right. It could do serious damage if I wasn't careful.

"You're right, I wasn't thinking. You know what, why don't you bring another sword and I'll use that instead tomorrow. Just to keep the danger to a minimum."

"You have a connection with this blade, Morgan, and you need to nurture it. I was simply not expecting your attack."

Before I could respond, my phone, which lay on the grass, buzzed with an incoming call from Julayne. I scooped it up and answered. "Jules, you're up early."

"Morgan, where are you? I went to your room and you're not there. You know today is important."

"Relax, I just went for a walk. I'll be back in a few minutes," I replied. Though as I finished my sentence, I heard a strange sound over the line.

Whatever Julayne was about to say next was swallowed by a high-pitched whining sound and then the line went dead.

TWO

I stared at my phone as my mind tried to work out what had just happened. The high-pitched whining still buzzed in my ears as Julayne's words registered in my brain. Today my mother would sign the peace treaty between Camelot and the Seelies. Thanks to Shunae and her diplomatic team's efforts, we'd reached an agreement with King Uther. We could avoid descending into war over the whole 'trying to murder me as a baby and install a false heir' fiasco. It had completely slipped my mind, even though it was all anyone had been talking about for weeks.

I glanced at Taron as he stowed his sword. Of course, I'd had other things on my mind at the time. He looked back at me with concern crinkling the skin around his eyes and mouth. "Everything all right?"

"Uh ... well, I totally forgot I'm due back at the castle for a big family thing." I trusted Taron, but I wasn't sure I should be divulging my kingdom's inner workings to him. He might be an ally, but you couldn't be too careful.

"You look a bit shaken for that to be the whole truth," he countered.

"I'm sure it's nothing." I glanced down at my phone and hit redial. The same high-pitched sound came from the line. Was it this world's version of a busy signal or something? "Think my phone's on the fritz again."

His brow furrowed and he dug into his belongings, producing a phone I'd never seen before. It was sleeker than mine and smaller. He tapped the screen a few times before holding it out to me. "Try using this."

I entered Julayne's number and dialed again, with the same result. I tried Gethin next. Still that horrible noise. So, it wasn't just my phone. An uneasy feeling settled over me, gripping my stomach tight and twisting. Something was off here.

"I should probably get going."

"I could take you back if you want."

I was not a fan of heights and yet I knew I'd be safe in Taron's embrace. And while I relished the thought of him disrobing again in order to shift into his dragon form for the trip, I knew it wasn't a good idea. We'd been keeping these mornings together private. And I wanted to keep it that way if possible.

"I'll be fine. Thanks though." I glanced at the phone still in my hand. "But if you wanted to give me your mobile number, I'd take it."

He smiled. "That I can certainly do."

I handed him my phone and he tapped away. When he handed the device back to me, I couldn't help but smile. He'd taken the liberty of identifying himself as Hot Dragon Prince. I snorted aloud in spite of myself. "Bit full of yourself, aren't you?"

"You were the one who accused me of being ... physically distracting."

He wasn't wrong. "Well, now I can get a hold of you in a pinch."

"Ah, so you will leave me unable to return the favor?"

I tapped his name on my phone's screen and placed the call. I expected to see it pop up on his screen as an incoming message, but that same damn noise filled the air. I ended the call quickly and frowned. "I guess we'll have to do this the old-fashioned way." I pocketed my phone and navigated to the contacts list on his device. I added myself in and handed it over.

"Well, that's disappointing." Taron gave me an exaggerated pout. "And here I had hoped you would have followed my naming convention."

"Leaving it to your imagination."

The pout faded into an easy smile. "Same time tomorrow then?"

"Assuming there's no grand catastrophe to intervene."

He offered me a bow and made like he was going to reach for my hand, but stopped himself. Was he about to kiss my hand? "Travel safe, Morgan." His voice was low, and I could swear there was a glint of orange around his irises when he straightened.

I moved a few paces down the lakeshore before lifting my hands to trace a circle in the air. As I did so, the scent of my magic—lime—filled my nose. It was hard to believe I'd been here for three months. Camelot really was starting to feel more like home. The amount of control I'd been able to gain in that short time was remarkable. Some days I still couldn't quite believe I was the same woman who'd struggled to even sustain a spell long enough to boil a kettle for tea. Now, I was creating portals like it was nothing.

The familiar slope of the castle grounds appeared within the circumference of my portal, and I glanced back one last time to see Taron watching me intently. He wanted to be sure I made it back to the castle before he went on his way. I gave him a small wave before stepping through and leaving the lake behind.

I'd made this trip more times than I could count since Jules had come to Camelot. Part of me felt a touch guilty for leaving her out of my morning excursions. But then, it wasn't like she had a reason to see Taron naked. I stepped through the portal onto hard, paved ground just beyond the outer wall of the castle. It was secluded enough, and security patrols usually passed it by while I was gone, so there was little risk of getting caught.

However, today the place was in chaos. Uniformed men and women darted around looking frazzled. One of them spotted me and made a beeline in my direction. I wanted to move, to get out of their way, but they backed me against a wall.

"You shouldn't be out here," he said in a gruff tone.

"I'm fairly certain I'm allowed to be wherever I want, thanks."

Frustration darkened his features. "You should be with the Queen at a time like this."

Without ceremony, he grabbed me by the forearm and hauled me away from the wall. I tried to shake him off, but his hand clamped like a vice around my bicep, squeezing tighter the more I struggled.

"Oi, let me go!" I snapped when he'd dragged me through the courtyard to the front doors of the castle.

His jaw worked like he wanted to offer a snarky retort, but he kept silent. Better for his health that he did. He opened the front door and shoved me unceremoniously over the threshold. Without giving me any more direction, he slammed the door shut at my back.

Prick.

That left me to stare at my surroundings in confusion. Something was definitely going on. Everyone looked so frantic they weren't interested in stopping to even notice me. Or maybe they still weren't used to my presence in the castle. In a way, I couldn't blame them. For three decades they'd spent their careers serving a man they thought would one day be king. Now, he'd proven to be the heir to the enemy's throne, shoved into my place in a bid for power.

Shaking off the unease, I made my way down the hall to my mother's sitting room. Most days I could find her there this early in the morning, sneaking a cup of espresso when she thought no one was looking. The room was in disarray, tea tray overturned, liquid spreading out in a dark pool on the carpet. I reached for my phone again before stopping myself. I had no reason to think the phones would work within the castle either.

That left the throne room or the Council Chamber. Given the chaos, I opted for the latter. Even before I'd made it halfway down the corridor, I could sense the tension in the space. The usual guards who monitored the doors were conspicuously absent. Whatever lay behind the doors was enough to need their presence elsewhere. I swallowed the sudden lump in my throat as I pushed the doors inward.

A full-on war room scenario spread out before me. My mother stood at the far side of the table, bent over a small computer, Shunae and a few other Council members crowded around her. Emerys and Julayne stood off to one side. Gethin was nowhere to be seen, although I suspected he was either still asleep or busy making breakfast down in the kitchen. Jules was the first to notice my presence and slunk around the perimeter of the room to reach me.

"Out for a walk?" she hissed.

"It's good for my health." I gestured to the cluster of people at the other end of the room. "What the bloody hell is going on? One minute you're on the line, the next there's this awful whining sound and nothing goes through."

"There's been an attack."

Emerys' sudden interjection to the conversation made me jump. "What sort of attack?"

"Cyber," Jules offered. "The whole network went down all at once. Internet, phones, all normal means of communication."

That was enough to draw my mother's attention. The stress lines around her eyes softened ever so slightly when she registered my presence. She waved me over and I left my companions to join her.

"This is going to sound ignorant, but we're in a realm full of magic. Dragons, fae, and someone is trying to cripple us with ... computers? Isn't that sort of mundane?"

"You have much to learn about our world," my

mother said. "So many of our systems are imbued with magic. As our civilization grew, so did the way in which we used magic to keep our world connected."

I bent to study the screen she was so focused on a moment ago. I hadn't been privy to many cyber assaults in my time—except the odd virus from surfing sketchy websites as a teen. Though even I couldn't deny the message flashing on the screen read as an attack.

Free those held unjustly in your prisons or suffer our wrath.

"Any idea what this is about?"

"After Arthur was unmasked, we discovered several Seelie sympathizers who had apparently aided him in concealing his identity," Shunae said. "They've been imprisoned pending trial."

"This is the Seelies?"

"It would certainly appear to be the case," Emerys interjected calmly.

"I'm assuming we don't negotiate with terrorists?"

"We do not," my mother answered firmly.

"So, what do we do? I mean, if they've taken out the whole communications network for the kingdom, we can't get the word out that we're even working on a fix."

"We're working to try and regain some control, but it will take time." The note of fear in my mother's voice came in stark contrast to Emerys' earlier statement.

"The timing isn't a coincidence," Shunae said.

"Right, the peace treaty going into effect."

"Doubt that's happening now," Jules said from the corner.

"She's not far off. Without an easy means of communication, it's wholly possible Uther will interpret our silence as a sign we are backing out of the deal."

"But if it's his people doing this, isn't he breaking the peace first?"

No one responded to my question. Another loud whining sound filled the space, and I clamped my hands over my ears to drown out the obnoxious tone. When it finally dissipated a little, the screen changed. Gone was the message demanding we free the Seelie sympathizers. The words filling the screen now were far worse:

Release the prisoners within five days or lose your kingdom forever.

"They can't believe we'll comply," I railed. "And

forgive me for saying this, but they went undetected for years here. What's stopping them from just pulling a jail break like Arthur did?"

My mother shot me a stern look and I realized not everyone in our present company might have been privy to the details of Arthur's escape. Emerys moved to stand at my side and placed a firm hand on my shoulder.

"The Queen has taken precautions to ensure such escapes could not be replicated."

"This is fucking ridiculous," I snapped. One of the older council members gave me an incredulous look and I shrugged. If he expected me to be a perfectly behaved princess, he had another thing coming.

Emerys tugged me away from the table. "I understand you're upset, but you must understand that there are certain expectations regarding your behavior."

"We're literally under attack. Some faceless arse-hole is threatening to destroy the entire kingdom and you're lecturing me about my language?"

"Give us the room." My mother's voice cut through the argument brewing between Emerys and I. Shunae opened her mouth to protest, but closed it a moment later, seemingly unable to disobey a directive from her queen. In short order everyone exited the room, leaving me and my mother alone.

"You aren't going to lecture me too, are you?"

"No. Quite frankly you voiced how I feel. I just don't have the luxury of saying it."

"I want to help, but I don't know how. I'm not great with computers."

She glanced at the screen as a glaring red counter ticked down the seconds under the hacker's deadline. "In truth, I'm not certain we will be able to regain control as easily as some might hope." She rubbed the bridge of her nose and brushed a few strands of greying hair out of her eyes.

"Tell me what I can do."

Before she could answer, I felt something warm against my breastbone and I reached beneath my shirt to reveal the compass the Crystal Cave had bequeathed me at the start of my first quest. The one that had brought Jules into my inner circle in this new world. It vibrated against my skin and when I opened it, the needle spun wildly, not settling in a direction.

"Has that happened before?"

I shook my head. We'd not really discussed my adventure back to London. Other than I was able to return the chalice back to Camelot and had a new companion in tow. She'd insisted it was safer that way. Still, I could read the longing in her glances sometimes. She wanted to be a part of my life after missing out on three decades of it. "It guided me last time, but it's been inactive for months."

"I am not an expert at reading signs from the universe, but I would say this might be one that you're meant to follow."

"Yeah, but follow it where exactly?"

"I think that is for you to determine."

I closed the top of the compass and tightened my hand around it. The connection of my fingers on the warm metal sent sudden shivers down my spine and the room around me vanished, replaced by the confines of the Crystal Cave. I could almost make out a voice calling to me, beckoning me. It would appear a new journey was upon me.

THREE

Part of me didn't want to believe the universe meant for me to leave Camelot *now*, not when it was in such dire straits. After all, its defenses and infrastructure were all but crippled from the cyber-attack. And in five days' time, the Seelies would descend. Uther hadn't gotten his hands on my mother's crown through his scheme with Arthur, so now he was resorting to brute force.

"I know that look." My mother's voice pulled me out of my rumination.

"What look? I don't have a look," I protested.

She smiled sadly. "It's one I've had many times myself. You don't want to go, but you know you have no choice."

"Don't I? I mean, I could just pretend I didn't see what I saw. You need me here."

She brushed a few strands of hair off my shoulder in a maternal gesture. "Yes, I want you here with me. That way, I know you are safe and protected." She glanced toward the closed door. "But realistically, there is little you can do here. And while we haven't known each other long, I suspect if you're anything like me, idleness drives you mad."

I hated that she had to quantify the length of our relationship. We should have had three decades to know one another. All that time to laugh at the fact that we shared the same looks. She also wasn't wrong that I hated sitting on my hands doing nothing.

"Won't it seem sudden, me just going off like this?" The last time I'd gone off to find the chalice, no one in Camelot had been aware of where I'd gone.

"As much as I hate to admit it, with our systems inoperable right now, no one is going to be aware of much of anything, I'm afraid."

"But we won't be able to stay in touch."

Her hand moved from my shoulder down past my elbow to settle on my wrist. She offered a light squeeze. "Then we will have to trust that you will return safely."

"Let's say I do go; I have no idea what I'm supposed to find."

"Magic has a way of making things clear right when we need it most. And I wouldn't let you go if you weren't accompanied."

As a teenager, if someone, even Nim, had said that to me, I'd have railed against the notion. I didn't need minding. But I had no intention of leaving the kingdom alone. If my trip back to London had taught me anything it was that I couldn't do this on my own. I needed help.

"I promise to come back. And when I do, it will be with help."

"We will be waiting." She glanced at the screen again with its ominous countdown. "But you need to hurry. I fear that those holding us hostage will not give us a moment's grace to meet their demands."

"Then I better get going." I pulled her into an unceremonious hug, grateful no one else was around to see how fiercely I clung to her.

After a beat, I relinquished my grip and moved to the door. I found Emerys and Jules waiting in the corridor a few paces away. Shunae and the other council members were conspicuously absent.

"We need to go," I announced to my friend and my mentor as the door to the chamber shut behind me.

"The kingdom's in a crisis, where do you suggest we go?" Julayne countered.

"Time for you to see the Crystal Cave," I whispered.

My words raised Emerys' brow in a surprised expression. "What draws you back there?"

I tapped the compass now hanging on the outside of my shirt. "I sort of had a vision. I think I'm meant to go there, but for what I'm not sure."

"We must tell Gethin."

I turned to Jules. "Can you pack us a week's worth of clothes while I go fill him in? We'll meet you by the side gate in ten minutes."

She looked ready to argue, but ultimately held her tongue. Emerys turned back toward the Council Chamber, as if unsure she wanted to leave my mother alone. Or was it unease about fearing I wouldn't ask her to join in?

"My mother knows I have to leave. And she's already told me I'm not allowed to go solo."

Her shoulders relaxed. "I will prepare a bag for Gethin and I. You should find him down in the kitchen."

I left them to their preparations as I wound my way to the kitchen. Either the news hadn't spread to the chefs, or they didn't need technology for their duties. The kitchen was humming with energy and the air was thick with the aroma of breakfast. Gethin stood at a counter kneading dough between his fingers.

"Morning," he greeted, glasses perched precariously on the bridge of his nose.

"Sorry to interrupt what I'm sure was going to be a delicious meal, but we need to go."

He stopped his work and turned to face me, managing to smear a bit of flour across one cheek as he adjusted his glasses. "What's going on?"

"You might not have noticed, but the whole kingdom's under attack. Some Seelie hacker has taken control of the whole system and is threatening war. Anyway, I have this feeling that we need to ... uh, take a little trip to the woods for some answers."

I caught one of the pastry chefs leaning in. No doubt they're hoping to catch some gossip to send around the castle. They backed off when I fixed them with a glare. Gethin looked poised to pepper me with questions. Instead, he wiped his hands on a rag, slid off his apron and started for the door.

"Uh mate, you've got a little something right there." I caught him before he could get far and pointed at his face.

He ran the back of his hand over his cheek in embarrassment—pink tinging his skin—before we headed toward the side entrance. He had the decency to wait until we were out of earshot to let loose with his questions.

"How do we know what happened? Are we sure it's a legitimate threat?"

"Looked pretty legitimate. Phones are down. Internet seems to be, too. Every way we have to get the news out to people is cut off. We're blind and mute."

"And why would a trip to the woods help?"

I tapped the compass again. "I don't know yet. But I have a feeling we're going to find out."

His eyes lit up as reality dawned on him. "Do you think we'll head back to London?"

"Your guess is as good as mine. Come on, we need to meet Emerys and Jules. We've only got five days before the shit hits the fan."

SLIPPING out of the castle was easier than I'd expected. Or maybe since I was in the company of the queen's advisor, the guards assumed I wasn't going to get into mischief. Oh, if only they knew. I led the way off the castle grounds before raising my hand in the air.

"Are you certain you can keep a portal steady?" Emerys looked genuinely concerned about my skill.

"I've been practicing," I answered and traced a circle in the air. The image of her cabin appeared neatly at the center, and I motioned a hand for my companions to step through. Jules went first, two bags slung over her shoulders. Gethin followed with Emerys bringing up the rear. I stepped through, letting the magic drop away the moment my feet were on the grass. The air around me zapped back together, taking the image of the castle's exterior wall with it.

"You have been practicing." Emerys sounded impressed.

"I am capable of learning, thank you very much," I muttered and started for the woods that concealed the cave.

"Have you eaten?" Gethin called, stopping me in my tracks.

"I appreciate your concern for my digestive health, but I think I can afford to skip breakfast," I retorted.

"Oh, come on, Morgan, you know breakfast is the most important meal of the day." Jules bumped my shoulder and gave me a smirk.

I let out a slow breath as my stomach gave a rebellious growl of hunger. All four of us didn't need to make the trek to the cave, especially not when I didn't know what awaited me. "Fine. We're here at the cabin. Why don't you fix us something to eat? And I promise we'll eat before we do anything else when I get back."

Gethin looked more relaxed as he veered off, pressing his hand to the front door of the cabin. I thought I heard the soft audible sigh it always gave when Emerys walked in. Apparently, the place had accepted Gethin as a permanent fixture, too.

"What did you see that has led you back to the cave?" Emerys asked as we made the trek across the hills to the woods that served as the barrier between this realm and the one, I'd called home for my entire life.

"I'm not sure really. I touched the compass and saw the cave. It almost sounded like someone was calling to me. I know that's not how it works, but it felt like that."

"The cave's offered many miraculous things over the centuries," she admitted with a wistful note in her voice.

Soon enough, we were picking our way through brambles. To my surprise the greenery was still in full bloom despite the weather turning cooler. Then again, I hadn't noticed the foliage around the cabin earlier. My trips here of late had been focused solely on the lake.

"So, how does this work? I mean, that looks pretty tiny." Jules gestured toward the mouth of the cave and then to the three of us.

"I suspect Morgan is meant to enter alone," Emerys answered.

"But what if she's not meant to go alone? Wouldn't it want us to have all the same information? Things can get lost in translation," she protested.

"Relax, Jules. You're not going to miss out on anything important. Maybe a bit of weirdness, but definitely nothing crucial."

I stepped up to the opening in the rough-hewn rock and pressed my left palm to the surface. The small sapphire at the bottom of Excalibur in bracelet form brushed against the stone and my entire body began to vibrate as if I were a tuning fork and someone had just struck me to find the right pitch.

I clenched my jaw as I walked inside, leaving Jules and Emerys to wait outside for me. I heard an indignant grumble as I turned back to see Jules trying to gain entry and the cave reacted to her attempted intrusion. I sensed a surge of power around me as the magic within this place kept her out, forcing her back.

"I'll be right back," I called, hoping I wouldn't be made a liar.

The cave looked as it had on each of my last visits with an impossible light illuminating the shallow pool at the back of the space and the precariously placed stalactites hanging overhead. I crouched in the cramped space as I moved to settle beside the pool of water and studied my reflection. She looked more settled somehow. Then again, I felt more at ease in this place even after just a few months. Albion was beginning to feel more like home by the day.

"I'm here. You have something to show me, so

let's get on with it. I don't know if you can perceive things like deadlines, but we're working against a bit of a tight one."

My voice echoed in the space, filling my ears. A part of me still felt ridiculous talking to myself like this. The tiny voice in the back of my head kept telling me that no one was actually going to answer back.

"Well, this is weird," an unfamiliar female voice called from across the pool.

Startled, I looked up to find a redhead in jeans and a leather jacket sitting cross-legged. A silver pentacle hung around her neck. Her bright green eyes were inquisitive, if a bit confused by her surroundings.

"Uh, come again?"

My voice caught her attention and she turned to me. "I didn't think I'd ever be back here. Well, not here exactly I guess since I have no idea where I am, but this plane of existence."

Her accent betrayed her as American. She looked young, a few years my junior maybe, but I could still sense that she was powerful.

"Sorry, I don't mean to be rude, but who are you?"

In the blink of an eye, she disappeared from her

spot across the water to reappear at my side, hand outstretched. "I'm Ezri Trenton."

The way she said her name suggested I ought to know her. But I'd never heard the name in my life. Still, I shook her outstretched hand. "Morgan le Fey." After a beat, I added, "What did you mean by this plane of existence?"

"Oh, I'm dead." Her face shifted into a mask of concern. "Don't freak out. It's okay really. It was supposed to happen."

Even though we'd never met before, I couldn't shake the sense that this dead woman was somehow familiar. I could almost see a hint of Emerys' coloring in her complexion. "So again, why are you here in my cave? Well, it's not *my* cave but ... oh, this was so much easier when I was just talking to my own reflection."

"Well, I guess the universe thought you could use my help. It's funny that way, sometimes. Though usually for me, it was all cryptic prophecy bullshit."

I let out a laugh. "I just get strange visions and hangout in magical caves."

"I bet it's a lot easier to decipher."

"Wouldn't bet on that." I was beginning to like

her. "I had a vision of the cave today and I suppose that was thanks to you?"

She shrugged. "I learned a long time ago that magic does what it wants and what it needs, to keep things balanced. If that means sending me here, who am I to argue?"

"Well, we're in a bit of a crisis and I need to find someone to help fix things before war breaks out."

"Yeah, I think I see why I'm here now."

"Care to fill me in then?"

"You're a hero," she said directly. "Or you're going to be."

"How do you know that?"

She gave me a knowing smirk. "Because I'm one, too. Or I was. Hence the whole destined to die thing. Anyway, I think I'm here to help point you in the right direction."

"No offense, but I've already got a magical guide, one who is very much alive. Nearly ancient, but alive."

"Oh, I know." She held up a hand to keep me quiet. "Don't ask, it will just hurt your head. The point is your journey's about to send you into my old stomping grounds and I couldn't let you go ... not without telling you that you shouldn't worry.

Where you're headed, you'll find plenty of allies, even if they don't seem like it at first."

"And where exactly are your stomping grounds?"

"Boston."

"Boston? As in America?"

"Yep."

Well, shit.

FOUR

Ezri stared at me, as if expecting me to say something else. My jaw worked to form words, but nothing came out. I swallowed, took a deep breath, and tried again. "I don't mean to come off as rude, but usually I come in here and get some hint as to what I'm meant to be looking for or do."

"Talk to strangers in caves often, then?" she quipped with a smirk.

"Well, not really. Like I said, usually I'm just talking to myself or get weird visions. Not normally seeing dead people."

"I'm not exactly sure what you're supposed to be looking for. I could just sense that where you are meant to go was where I've been and the people I left behind might be wrapped up in it."

"No inkling at all? Last time, I ended up finding the actual Holy Grail."

She stared at me, mouth slack and eyes wide. "For real?"

I nodded. "Hidden by some dragons who brought it through a portal to another world with my like eight times great grandfather."

"Damn." She sounded genuinely impressed.

"And not to rush you or anything, but we've got a bit of a ticking clock. Some crazy lunatics have taken over our entire communications network and they're threatening to start a war in five days if we don't give them what they want."

"Deadlines like that suck. Believe me, I've come up against a few myself." She got a wistful glint in her eye. Part of me wanted to dig for the details, but my gut told me now wasn't the time.

The look faded and she turned back to me, her expression serious. "When you've gotten these visions before, how did it happen?"

I tapped the compass around my neck. "This usually gives me a hint."

She made a grabbing gesture, and I leaned forward so she could reach it. The moment her fingers wrapped around the compass, the scent of lime flared around me, tinged with something sweet, like strawberry and the cave fell away.

Images of a cityscape flew by all around us, and a blur of faces skipped along as if someone had put a video on fast forward. In the chaos I thought I spotted something glittering and pale pinkish purple. It must have caught Ezri's attention too, because I could sense her trying to slow things down. The smell of berries grew stronger, and I could almost taste it on my tongue as the scene stopped rushing by and I could get a clearer image of what looked to be a necklace. Who owned it or where I might find it was still a blur. But at least I had an idea of what I was meant to look for now.

Ezri's fingers released her grip on the cool metal around my neck and the scent of strawberry ebbed away. The citrus of my own magic hung heavy in the air as I tried to catch my breath. The cave walls came back, as if closing in around me and I gasped for air.

"Easy." Ezri's voice was gentle, and I felt her hand on my shoulder, trying to steady me.

I squeezed my eyes shut to block out my surroundings for a moment. Taking a deep breath, my heartbeat settled back into a normal rhythm and the sudden panic from feeling like I was about to be closed in faded.

"Never had that happen before," I finally managed and opened my eyes again.

"I didn't know if it would do anything."

"Definitely did something all right. I guess I'm meant to find some sort of necklace."

"Looked like it, yeah." Her brow furrowed for a moment before smoothing out again. "I don't know if it's going to be the answer, but I've got a friend there who is pretty handy with computers and magic. You should at the very least look her up."

"Great. What's her name?"

"Avery Fellowes. It might sound weird at first, but tell her I sent you."

I had an object and a name. It was more to go on than I had even a few minutes ago. I caught Ezri eyeing me pensively. "You have something else to say?"

She shrugged. "Magic always has a reason for doing what it does. We don't always see it in the moment, but it's there. I'm just trying to figure out why the universe thought we needed to have this little chat."

"You said it yourself; I'm heading to your city, and it seems to have wanted me to know who to look for to start digging."

She bit her lower lip. "Yeah, but it feels bigger than that. Deeper somehow."

"Wish I knew."

"I'm sure it will all make sense eventually. You should go. Like you said, you've got that ticking clock. Good luck Morgan."

"Thanks."

I watched as the redhead stood and disappeared into the water without so much as a ripple, leaving me once more alone with my reflection in the cave. The crystals above me twinkled. I could swear they had that same pinkish-purple hue as the necklace I was meant to find.

Rising as much as I could in the cramped quarters, I shuffled back to the cave's entrance. Emerys and Jules were still waiting for me. I let out a sigh when I could straighten to my full height and relished the open space around me.

"So, did you find out anything?" Jules asked the moment she spotted me.

"I did. It's going to take some planning, but we're headed across the pond."

"I'm afraid I do not follow." Emerys couldn't hide her confusion.

"We have to go to America," I clarified. Before either of them could say anything else, I started through the brush and back toward the cabin. "Come on, brainstorming our plan of attack will go better with whatever Gethin's cooked up for us."

EMERYS' cabin smelled heavenly as we walked in. Gethin paced the distance from the entry to the kitchen to the bottom of the stairs. He stopped as the door eased shut behind us. I caught the tension in his shoulders visibly slacken, when he registered, we were back.

"That was not a quick trip to the cave," he said and practically shoved me toward the table laden with crepes, fruit tarts, and scones. I spotted some poached eggs and sausages on a platter too.

"Sorry, it got a bit complicated." I settled in a seat and began loading up my plate.

"Except you still haven't told us what you saw." Jules sounded like she needed a good meal, too, to temper her hunger.

I looked at Emerys, who'd remained quiet since we started our walk back. "You ever spoken with a dead person in there before?"

She smiled and a hint of sadness tugged at the edges of her expression. "Not in a long time."

'But it's possible?"

"Yes."

"Good, so I wasn't going mental, then."

"Did you talk to Nim?" Jules' voice grew softer as she spoke my aunt's name.

"No. Though as much as I miss her and wish I could talk to her again, it's probably a good thing it wasn't her. I'm not sure I'd have been able to bring myself to leave otherwise."

"Who did you speak with?" Emerys joined us at the table.

"A woman named Ezri. She was American. Said that we were headed to her old stomping grounds, and she thought I should know that we've got potential allies there."

"I'm not familiar with your world's geography. Is that close to where we were last time?" Gethin nudged his glasses up the bridge of his nose.

"No. It's another continent."

"I see now why you thought we ought to contemplate our next steps," Emerys noted around a bite of sausage.

"Can't you just portal us there?" Jules eyed me over the top of her coffee mug.

"Well, I could get us to London for sure. But

America is a whole different place. I've only been there once and not where we need to be."

"Where would it put us?" Gethin leaned forward, chin propped on his hand.

"New York." I turned to Jules. "But you've been there a lot more than I have. You spent an entire school term there, remember? You sent me post-cards from all the places you visited. Wasn't one of them Boston?"

Jules' face paled a bit. "That was so long ago, Morgan. I mean, sure I went places, but I wasn't really focused on charting the terrain or anything."

"But if it's in your head, you could pull it out again. Come on, Jules."

"I just don't feel comfortable. And it's not like I've been practicing portal making. With you and Emerys around, I think we've got that particular skill covered."

"We could attempt to revive the memory through magic and allow Morgan to see it. It could be enough to get us where we need to be." Emerys arched a brow at both of us. "I believe that is some-thing within both of your skill levels."

If we'd still been in London and she'd never come to take me home, I wouldn't have been able to do a damn thing to get us across an ocean. I still marveled about how much stronger my magic had become in such a short time. It wouldn't have been even three months ago when I arrived in Albion.

"I say we at least give it a go," I said, fixing Jules with what I hoped was a supportive look.

"What if it doesn't work? What if I can't remember it in enough detail? We could end up landing in a river or the middle of a building or something."

I reached across the table and squeezed her hand. "Then we'll find another way. But we need to try this first."

"Fine. We can try." She sounded almost defeated.

I hated imposing on my friend, but I needed her now. Even if she was scared, which felt a little unlike my best friend. She was one of the most fierce and fearless people I knew. I let silence fall as we all focused on our breakfast.

A short while later, I let Emerys and Gethin clear the dishes away as I led Jules upstairs to the room, I briefly had called my own when I'd first arrived. "I've done this before, it's best to get comfortable."

"I'm afraid I'm going to fail," she blurted.

"Jules, you are one of the strongest, most gifted witches I've ever met. You can do this."

"But what if I *can't*."

I guided her to the bed. "What's gotten into you? I've never seen you this unsure of yourself, especially when it comes to magic."

"I don't know." She studied her nails. "I thought when we came here, it would just be magical, like Nim described. But I see how much you've grown here, and I guess I feel a little left out."

"We knew I'd be doing important things when I came here." I'd admit, I hadn't expected to keep going off on quests with such alarming frequency, but at least I knew I had a place to return to.

"Maybe I'm just feeling a bit untethered from my magic. Like how you were cut off from yours for so long."

I hadn't stopped to consider that the predicament I'd lived with for thirty years might befall my best friend. "I hadn't thought of that. I'd assumed that because you were meant to be in this with me that the universe would make it so you'd be able to use your powers, too."

"Do you hate me for feeling so weak?"

"I could never hate you, Jules. I'm sorry I didn't see what you were going through." After a beat I added, "If you really aren't comfortable with this, we can find another way."

She sucked in a big breath. "No. We can try, I just don't want you to be disappointed if it doesn't work."

"I promise I won't be." I took her hands in mine and closed my eyes. "Now, picture the last time you were in Boston. Every sight, smell, and sound you can recall. Hold it in your head like a picture. Then I'll try to pull it out of you, so I can see it."

Jules settled back against the pillows, and I waited for her to give some sort of signal that she'd recalled the memory we needed. Her brows knit together, and her eyes darted back and forth beneath her eyelids as I waited.

"I think I've got it," she whispered.

I tightened my grasp on her hands and poured a little of my own magic into the mix. The sharp taste of lime tickled the back of my tongue as I willed whatever she saw to fill the space around us. The walls flickered, briefly replaced by the cacophony of a city street. Tall buildings of glass and steel rose up, disappearing into the ceiling overhead. Nothing in these surroundings screamed Boston. But then again, I'd never been there myself so I couldn't judge.

"Keep going," I urged, squeezing her hands tighter.

"I'm giving it everything I've got."

I focused more power into the connection between us, silently begging the magic that bound all living things together to give us this win. The cityscape sputtered before solidifying and an open green space sprawled out through the window over-looking the lake.

"What is this place?" My voice came out strained as I did my best to focus on fueling the spell.

"It's uh ... downtown."

I tried to commit the image to memory, but if I was honest, I didn't feel confident that I could get us there safely. It felt too public and while there were tall stands of trees that lined the paths that wound their way through the greenery, I didn't trust that our group popping out of thin air wouldn't attract some level of attention. Besides, we didn't need any help being noticed.

I was the first to break the connection, Julayne's memory fading from the space around us. She opened her eyes and they sparkled with unshed tears. I pulled her wordlessly into a hug.

"You did brilliant. But I don't think I'm good enough to get us there," I whispered against her hair cascading over one shoulder in a loose plait.

"So, what do we do now?"

I pulled away and shook my head. "I don't know, but we'll figure it out together."

"We better go down and tell them that we're going to need a Plan B."

She wasn't wrong. Setting off on this quest was proving to be more complicated than I'd expected. And I couldn't shake the dread settling around my chest at the promised threat of losing our entire kingdom. My people's very existence was riding on our success.

I half-expected to find Gethin eavesdropping by the door, but he and Emerys were nowhere to be seen. I descended the stairs to find the eating area cleaned up and the kitchen empty. The front door was still closed. We would have heard them if they'd been on the second level. So, that left one place to look: the training area. I led the way to the space that at first glance looked like the rest of the flora in the area. Tall trees stood with their branches reaching high toward the sky. Gethin stood at the far end of the space. Well, standing wasn't the right word. Hovering better described the fact that his feet didn't touch the dirt.

"What's he doing?" Jules' voice carried to fill the space.

I could swear the branches overhead bent down, as if listening to her words. Gethin's eyes shot open, and his feet hit the ground with a scuffing sound. "Did you get it figured out?"

"Not exactly. I mean, Jules was able to recall a memory and I could project it around us. But honestly I don't think I'm good enough yet to get us there without sending us into a tree."

"So, we need to find another way there," Jules proposed.

"Emerys thought you might."

I didn't love that my supposed mentor doubted my skills. Sure, I could doubt myself from here until the sun froze. I'd been doing it my entire life. But it stung that Emerys didn't believe in me enough to think I could be able to do it.

"Is that why she's not here?" Jules moved to perch on one of the stumps near the farthest tree.

"She went back to Camelot to confer with the queen."

Another pang of irritation tightened my chest. I knew I was being a jealous twat. She and my mother could have a relationship that didn't include or revolve around me. At the very least she could have waited to see the outcome of our efforts first.

"Are we supposed to stay here until she gets back then?" I didn't move from where I stood opposite Gethin.

"She didn't actually say."

"Great. Then she won't mind if I pop back for a chat," I said and pivoted to head back inside.

"Morgan, I'm sure she will come back," Gethin called.

"Let her go," Jules replied. "Don't worry, I'll keep you company."

I heard Gethin give an audible swallow as I sketched a circle in the air in front of me, picturing my mother's sitting room. The warmth of the space coupled with the inviting armchairs filled the opening and I stepped through.

Both my mother and Emerys looked surprised when I materialized, the portal snapping shut behind me. They sat side by side around a small table with a pen and paper between them.

"I instructed Gethin to let you know I would return shortly," Emerys noted.

"Didn't feel like waiting. And no offense ... actually yeah, some offense, you didn't bother to wait to see if I could handle the spell before you got a backup plan?"

"You have progressed so much since you came back, but three months of being in the place you're meant to be doesn't make up for three missed decades working against you," my mother replied gently.

"Are you able to portal us to where we need to go?" Emerys looked at me, an expectant look arching her right eyebrow.

"No."

"Then I would say it is fortuitous that we are already seeking an alternative."

My mother waved her hand and another chair skittered across the carpet to join them. "Sit."

I sunk into the chair and studied the elegant script on the page that read: *photo, date of birth and residence.* "You're talking about creating a fake ID."

My mother grinned. "I knew she'd understand."

I looked at Emerys. "When we met, you mentioned not having time to forge documents. This is something you've considered before."

"At that time, we did not have the luxury of a few hours to prepare what we would need to make them convincing."

"But we do now?"

"Indeed, you do," my mother answered, and I caught a mischievous glint in her eye. "It is a little-known skill, and I would trust you to keep it that way, but I have a knack for copying ... art shall we say."

I couldn't help myself, I let out a bemused snort. "The queen is good at making forgeries?"

"In a sense," she answered. "I enjoyed art in my youth and have an eye for emulating style—"

"The problem is, we do not have something to compare," Emerys interjected.

"Well, if we're going to America, we'll need passports. And lucky for you I remembered to grab mine before we left after Nim's death."

"Then you should retrieve it. We will finish preparing what we can here," my mother said, making a shooing gesture in my direction.

I left the sitting room behind, making the now familiar trek to my bedroom. The halls had quieted down some in our absence. I was grateful there weren't security personnel eyeing me, judging me for daring to be anywhere in the castle without an escort. I found my passport in the drawer of the night table beside the bed where I'd left it. I flipped through it, noting the lack of stamps. I'd barely traveled, save for that single trip to New York to visit Jules while she was studying abroad.

"Guess you're about to get some serious use," I

muttered and tucked it in my pocket before retreating to the sitting room.

"Right, so you ought to use my address. Or maybe Jules'," I said as I walked in.

"Why?" My mother glanced at me as I set the passport on the table in front of her.

"Because if you make up an address, you risk someone at the airport knowing something's off. They aren't going to question it, if they've got a couple of people traveling with the same address."

"She makes a good point," Emerys noted, opening the document and jotting down my address.

"Not that I'm doubting your skills, but you can't just take a regular piece of paper and change it into something like this."

My mother smiled and set a pocket-sized item on the table beside my passport. "Lucky for us all, we carry similar identification. We may not travel through the barrier often, but it would seem many things from your world have bled into ours."

Far more than the other way around, that's for sure.

"Right, well should I just leave you to it and see you back at the cabin?"

"It won't take long to complete the spell," my mother answered before Emerys could speak.

I couldn't lie. I was eager to see my mother work this magic. In the time I'd known her, I'd never seen her do much magic at all. I could sense on a deeper level that she had it, like I could with Jules or Gethin, but she'd never felt the need to flaunt it. Until now.

She opened my passport and laid it as flat as she could on the table. Next, she opened the identification from Camelot—I could see our coat of arms and motto emblazoned on the front in silver foil stamping—to reveal my mother's photo. It had to be at least a decade old. She had fewer strands of grey in her hair and her face was a little thinner.

"Would you be so kind as to take a photograph of Emerys with your phone?"

"Why don't you have one of your own?" I eyed Emerys in confusion.

"I haven't had reason to travel amongst the kingdoms in a long while. I suppose I'm outdated in that regard."

I glanced around the room and pointed to a bare patch of wall. "That should be okay." It wasn't quite the boring grey-blue background they had in most official photo IDs, but it would have to do.

Emerys dutifully stood and stared at me while I captured her image on my phone. My finger hovered over the prompt to forward the image when I realized I had no way of sending it to my mother.

"Just give it here," she prompted and patted beside my open passport on the table.

I set the phone down and watched as my mother pressed her right index finger to the screen and her left to the image on the ID. Slowly, my mother's features shifted, taking Emerys' younger appearance. Her hair shimmered, taking on reddish hues instead of brown.

"Bloody brilliant," I murmured under my breath.

"I'm not done yet," my mother said with a note of confidence in her tone.

The text shifted next, changing to my address and Emerys' pertinent physical details. I marveled as the date of birth jumped and couldn't help but wonder if the date she'd chosen was accurate at least as to the month and day. No one would believe if it said she were 800 years old.

"Nearly there." My mother's forehead creased as she turned the two IDs over, so the outsides lay flat.

First the front covers and then the backs changed to match mine. When she pulled her hands away, I could see the sweat popping out along her hairline. I picked up the forged passport and looked it over.

"Yeah, I think this will do." After a moment, a thought occurred to me. "We're going to need one for Gethin."

"I'm afraid that's all I have in me right now," my mother admitted.

I wasn't going to push her. And as much as I wanted Gethin along with us, getting three people across an ocean was going to be difficult enough. I looked at Emerys. "I'm not breaking the news to him."

She picked up the ID and stowed it in a pocket before handing my passport over to me. "I will address that. You and Julayne should prepare to leave. Pack her a bag and we'll be on our way."

She didn't need to add that time was of the essence. I offered my mother a hug. "I promise, we'll be back with something that's going to fix this whole mess."

"I know you're going to try."

There wasn't time to let her words sting me. I left them alone again and retreated first to my room and then to Julayne's, double checking that we had enough clothing for four days. I refused to pack for a fifth, because we weren't going to be gone that long. There was simply no other option. I found Emerys waiting for me outside the sitting room, a pack slung over her shoulder as well.

"We're going to have to wait until we're in London to get plane tickets to Boston," I reminded her.

"Then we should get Julayne and depart immediately."

WE RETURNED to the cabin to find Jules and Gethin sparring in the outside training room. Gethin was hanging upside down from a string of leaves wound around his ankle. His glasses sat in the dirt beneath him. I couldn't help but snicker.

"Sorry to break up the party, but we've got a Plan B, and we need to get going."

Jules waved her hand. The leaves released their grip on Gethin, righting him so he didn't come crashing down head-first. He scooped up his glasses, reseating them on his nose. "So, what's the plan?"

"We're going to portal to London and catch a flight out to Boston," I explained, eyeing Jules. "You're going to need your passport."

"Then I guess we'll be portaling to my flat," she replied. Unlike Nim and I, Jules owned her flat outright. No fear of angry landlords coming around for overdue rent.

"How are we going to get through their identification measures?" Gethin directed his question to Emerys.

"I am afraid *we* won't. I was only able to secure identification for myself. But Her Majesty has assured me that she can use your skills at the castle. From what I've heard, the staff have come to rely heavily on your culinary gifts."

Gethin's cheeks flushed momentarily before he straightened. "Right. I can do that."

I could read the disappointment in his face, but his tone didn't waver or betray any of that emotion. Emerys waved a hand and a portal opened up in front of Gethin, leading to his room at the castle. "We will return before the deadline."

"You better." He stepped through and the opening closed with a soft 'pop.'

That left the three of us standing surrounded by tall trees and pale blue sky. I was going to miss this place. Still, I couldn't deny a sense of excitement about this quest leading us to a new place.

"Right, here we go."

We left the cabin behind and started for the woods that would eventually take us to and through the barrier back into the world I'd grown up in. While I knew I could portal us to Jules' flat, I couldn't do it from this side of the gate. The trek through the brambles and brush felt like second nature now. The shift as we passed from Albion into Ireland wasn't as drastic as it had been the first few times. Maybe the worlds were getting used to me passing from one to the other. Before long we found ourselves at the bottom of the shallow incline.

"This should be good," I said, halting my companions before they started up the hill.

My nerves jangled as I traced a circle in the air. I pictured Jules' flat. I could see the table in the front room, the small kitchen off to the corner, and the front window that overlooked the street. For a split second the image of one of the Seelie soldiers Uther had dispatched to kill me and Nim flashed through my mind. Somehow, I banished him from my mind and focused on the place that had always felt like a second home to me.

When I opened my eyes, the familiar image greeted me through the circular confines of my spell. I nodded towards Emerys and Jules. "After you."

Jules shouldered one of the bags I'd brought and stepped through. I thought I heard her give a sigh of relief to be back in familiar surroundings as she moved out of the way. Emerys followed after her, her feet landing softly on the hardwood. That left me standing in the clearing alone. I cast one last look at the open space of Uisneach before moving through myself, letting the magic fade behind me. We were one step closer to finding the pendant and the allies who could hopefully keep my kingdom and my people safe.

SIX

Making our way to Heathrow hadn't been hard. Jules had protested at the idea of taking a cheap airline, but we had limited time and didn't need to worry about checked luggage. So, I booked the earliest flight I could that got us into Boston six hours from now. It was time we weren't going to get back, but I had to believe we could still find the necklace and return to Camelot in five days or less to save the kingdom.

As we waited to board, I caught Emerys staring out the floor-to-ceiling windows. I nudged her shoulder to get her attention. "You aren't scared of confined spaces, are you?"

She offered me a small smirk. "No." After a moment, she added, "I was thinking that until I'd stepped through the barrier from this world into Albion for the first time so many centuries ago, I had never left my homeland. I had never dreamed of the world beyond my small corner of existence. However, I find myself filled with a sense of anticipation. I have never been to Boston and yet I feel as though it calls to me."

"Maybe you can sense what's waiting for us in America," I suggested as an announcement on the loudspeaker overhead blared that it was our zone's turn to board.

We joined Jules in line and waited to hand over our boarding passes. The woman at the ticket counter eyed us and our light packs skeptically before waving us down the jetway and onto the plane. Given the late purchase of our tickets, I was surprised that we'd gotten decent seats in the middle of the plane. We stood in an awkward cluster blocking the aisle as we tried to sort out who would sit where.

"Jules, you go to the window. I'll take the middle and Emerys can have the aisle," I insisted. I felt the irritated glares of the other passengers waiting to board as we clogged up the flow of foot traffic.

Jules scooted past the armrests and settled against the window. I sat beside her, and Emerys took the spot along the aisle. In short order, everyone had boarded, and I buckled my safety belt, tuning out the speech about safety procedures. I was vaguely aware of Emerys hanging on the flight attendant's every word.

Blood rushed in my ears as the plane took off and my temples throbbed painfully as we left London behind. Even though it was still morning, I felt an urge to sleep and found it almost impossible to keep my eyes open once the plane reached cruising altitude.

"You should rest while you have the time," Emerys whispered in my ear, somehow cutting through the thrum of the plane's engines.

"Just a little nap," I murmured.

The world around me shifted, replacing the interior of the plane with a bustling cityscape I only vaguely recognized. That same hint of strawberry I'd sensed before from the cave tickled the edges of my senses, like Ezri was still trying to guide me. Everything looked frozen in place, like a video where I still needed to hit 'Play.' As if by thinking it, the world around me started moving. Mercifully, it went at normal speed. I could make out tall glass-fronted buildings and heard the screech of what sounded like wheels on a track in the distance.

The image jumped and suddenly there were other buildings, stout brownstones and that same span of green with the paths running through it. A gold-domed building sat behind me with a set of stairs leading up to it. It meant nothing to me and yet I could tell it was important. I felt drawn to the grassy area and in the blink of an eye, I stood on one of the grassy expanses. I couldn't explain why, but a shiver danced down my spine as I stood there, taking in the cool late autumn air.

Footsteps sounded behind me, and I pivoted to see a woman moving away from me. Her blonde hair bounced against her shoulders as something like headphones hung around her neck. She turned just enough for me to discern glasses framing her face as she watched me in profile. Sunlight glinted off something small nestled against her breastbone. Before I could reach out to get her attention she vanished.

"Morgan, wake up," Jules called, her voice was too loud.

I opened my eyes to find Jules leaning over me, concern etched into her normally angular facial features. I tried to straighten in the seat and found my right hand clasped tight around the compass. "How long was I out?" My mouth felt stuffed with cotton as I spoke.

"We just landed," she answered.

I sat up straighter, releasing my grip on the compass. "I slept the whole flight?"

"You looked rather peaceful, and we did not want to rouse you until we had no other choice," Emerys answered.

I wanted to share the dream with them both. It was still vivid in my head, but a crowded plane was not the place for this conversation. I undid the safety belt buckle and tugged my pack from beneath the seat in front of me. "Let's go. The sooner we get through Customs, the better."

By the time we'd disembarked and found our way to Customs, the dream started to fade. I considered forcing another vision from the compass, but didn't need any officials taking notice. The line ahead of us inched forward. No time like the present.

"I dreamt about what I saw in the cave again," I said.

"The dead woman?" Emerys prodded.

"No. Although, it felt like she was still there, guiding me somehow. But I saw the city. And a different woman. I think she might have had the necklace we're after."

"And did you get a feeling like this woman

would just hand it over, so we can get back through the barrier fast?" Jules pressed.

"She was gone too quickly. But I think we need to figure out where I saw her."

"Next," a burly man behind the counter called and I moved to stand in front of him. He studied the customs form Jules must have filled out for me while I slept, along with my passport.

"How long are you planning to be here Miss, uh ... le Fey?"

"Only a few days. Just a brief tourist trip. Showing some friends the city," I answered.

He glanced behind me, then stamped my passport, and gestured for me to head through a corridor that ended up depositing me in baggage claim. A few minutes later, Emerys and Jules joined me. We stood there looking like the lost tourists we very clearly were.

"Did you see any other landmarks that might signal our destination?" Emerys asked, starting to walk towards an information booth.

"There were a bunch of brownstone buildings. And this one that had a gold domed roof. It looked important."

"Sounds like the State House," the woman in the information kiosk interjected pleasantly.

"Right, the State House," I said, trying to act like I'd simply forgotten the words. "You wouldn't happen to know how we could get there?"

"Sure." She pulled out a metro map and unfolded it. "You're going to want to catch the Silver Line towards South Station. Then it's just two stops on the Red Line and that'll put you at Park Street Station. The State House is just on the other side of the Common."

I plastered a smile on my face and accepted the map, acting like any of those words meant a bloody thing to me. "Thanks so much."

She pointed toward a machine farther down the baggage claim. "You can buy passes there." She then leaned in the other direction and gestured at a set of automatic double doors. "The bus picks you up out there."

"Thanks," I said, leading our trio towards the machine she'd indicated.

"Anyone remember to change over their currency?" Jules asked.

"Damn it," I groaned as I stared down at the five pound note I'd pulled from my bag.

"It accepts cards," the woman at the kiosk called.

Jules nudged me out of the way and proceeded to make the purchase on her credit card. She handed us flimsy printed cards as the machine spat them at her and we were off again.

THE SUN WAS ALMOST DIRECTLY OVERHEAD by the time we stepped out of the station at Park Street. I looked around, trying to gauge our surroundings from the cave vision and the dream from the plane. I hadn't seen anything like what sprawled before us, and yet there was an odd sense of familiarity about the place.

"Is that the State House?" Emerys pointed to the glitter of gold up an incline.

"Only one way to find out." I led the way along a straight path that brought us to a set of stairs. I bounded up them two at a time and stopped. "Yeah, this sort of looks right."

I turned my back to the gold-topped building and cast my gaze down at the greenery below. I didn't see any blonde women sporting headphones in close proximity. That would have been too simple. Time to rely on a little magic.

I pressed my left hand to the compass hanging around my neck and poured a little intent out, grateful to feel the power course through me with ease. Every time we crossed through the barrier, I couldn't help but worry the connection I'd finally found to my magic would disappear again.

Show me where to go.

The citrus scent of my magic filled the air around me and the compass warmed beneath my palm. I felt a strange sensation begin to vibrate up my arm, settling uncomfortably in my elbow. I looked down at the tiny sapphire in the bracelet around my wrist as it sparkled in the sunlight. It was as if Excalibur was trying to lend support. If we'd been anywhere else, I would have considered unsheathing the blade and letting it act as a divining rod, much as it had done the day Arthur had pulled his prison break. But we were in public, in a foreign city where we didn't know how much people knew about magic. We couldn't risk landing me behind bars for brandishing a weapon.

The sword seemed to sense my apprehension and the thrumming in my elbow faded. Blowing out a breath I refocused on the compass and a vaguely green aura filled the air ahead—leading us back down the steps and into the Common.

"This way," I announced and descended the stairs.

Emerys and Jules fell into step beside me as I

followed the near-invisible trail of magic along one of the paved paths that led into the heart of the space. I kept glancing at the pedestrians passing by, but none of them remotely resembled the bespectacled woman from my dream. Still, the more we walked, the warmer the compass grew against my fingers.

"We must be getting closer," I said as I pulled my hand away. The metal was too hot to touch with my bare skin now and I was grateful that my shirt provided some protection from the heat.

A shout filled the air around us, drowning out the ambient noise of conversations and the nearby flow of traffic.

"Get off me!" A distinctly feminine voice demanded from up ahead.

Without thinking, I took off at a run. The air around me parted, as if to give me a straighter path to the commotion. I stopped to find a woman wearing glasses, struggling with a masked man. He had his hands wrapped around her throat and I could see the color beginning to drain from her cheeks.

"Oi, let her go you perv!" I howled.

Power coalesced in my right palm, forming a solid mass and I lobbed it overhand at the man's back. It collided between his shoulder blades with enough force to make him loosen his grip. The woman, for her part, slammed her knee between his legs. He let out a pained grunt as his hands pulled away from her body. I thought I caught the glitter of something in the sunlight as he went down, but couldn't be certain what I'd seen. The man recovered faster than I'd have expected. The woman had started to back away, rubbing at her throat when he straightened, and I caught the glint of a switchblade in his hand. The way he waved it from side to side turned my stomach. This man had come prepared to do real damage.

"Run!" I shouted at the woman as I closed the distance between us.

Except she didn't move as he made a lunge for her. Somehow, he narrowly avoided cutting her. *Why isn't she getting the fuck out of here?* Her attacker shuffled back a pace or two and prepared to strike again. I flung caution to the wind and charged forward, throwing my weight into him as I tackled him to the ground. In hindsight I should have thought this plan through. He thrashed beneath me, and I struggled to stay on top of him, pinning him down.

We'd landed on solid pavement, and I could feel

the coarse surface through my jeans as I scrambled to maintain dominance. Out of the corner of my eye, I spotted a patch of grass. My magic leapt to attention as a thought formed. From what I could see, the man beneath me was purely mortal. And that meant if I could restrain him with a bit of nature, he had less chance of breaking the spell. I stretched out my hand, urging the roots to grow and extend toward me.

"Morgan!" Emerys' voice strained behind me.

I was about to turn and ask what happened when a piercing hot sensation ripped through my abdomen. In a split second, the man shoved me off and I tumbled onto my back, the sky filling my vision as my head connected painfully with the pavement. I bit my tongue and my mouth filled with the taste of blood. I still couldn't quite process what had happened until I saw the man scramble away, taking off out of my field of vision.

"Oh my God," the woman rasped, her face appearing above me. It greyed at the edges.

I coughed as blood dripped down my throat and I did my best to avoid spitting it out all over my shirt. I wanted to roll onto my side to clear my throat, but my body refused to obey my mind's commands.

"Try not to move. I'm going to get help." The woman disappeared from view, replaced instantly by Emerys.

Worry clouded her features, and I could see unshed tears threatening to fall. In all the time I'd known her, I'd never seen her get emotional. Not even when I'd suffered multiple broken bones in my bout against Arthur.

"Th-that was foolish," she chided, her voice cracking.

I had just enough control over my body to move my hand to feel the shaft of the switchblade protruding from my stomach before I passed out.

SEVEN

I couldn't say how long I'd been unconscious. But when the world did come back to me, all I could feel was throbbing pain and nausea. My head ached and my tongue stuck to the roof of my mouth with congealed blood. I was vaguely aware of movement around me.

"You said you were getting help." Jules' voice sounded distant and panicked.

"I did. Trust me, your friend is going to be in good hands."

Part of me wanted to join in the conversation, but I couldn't rouse myself enough to even open my eyes. So instead, I laid there, not moving as each breath made my belly sear with pain. Something akin to a moan must have escaped me, because I picked up on the rustling of fabric.

"Hold fast, Morgan. Help is coming." The touch of a hand accompanied Emerys' words.

Sirens wailed in the distance, growing louder and more insistent. I fought to at least open my eyes, but the world around me was blinding. I squeezed them shut again just as fast. Even with the brief glimpse, I could only make out blurred faces standing over me. The noise of the sirens was nearly deafening now, accompanied by the crunch of tires on pavement. Air brakes squealed and then footsteps followed.

"Avery, what the hell happened?" a male voice demanded.

"This guy came out of nowhere and she fought him off."

I detected an unmistakable sense of familiarity between the two speakers. With more determination this time, I cracked one eyelid to see a new blurry face hovering over me. "Hi there, my name's J.T. I'm going to help you."

An undecipherable groan passed my lips in response. He didn't seem to mind. He shined a small pen light in my partially open eye. I raised my hand to block the painful intrusion.

"He's just trying to make sure you aren't concussed," Jules said, reaching to keep my hand out of his way.

"I know it's uncomfortable, I'm sorry." J.T.'s voice was soothing.

Maybe it was the blood loss, but I relaxed and even managed to open my other eye without wanting to pass out again. I tolerated the light and as he leaned back, my vision cleared.

"Can you tell me your name?" He reached for my left wrist, gripping it just below where the sapphire sat nestled against my pulse point.

Before I had a chance to answer him, a rush of power erupted from my left hand. The bracelet shifted, Excalibur materializing in its full form. J.T. skittered back as the blade hovered in front of me, as if an invisible entity held it in a defensive posture.

"He's not trying to harm you," Emerys said.

"Not .... me," I managed through the mess of blood and saliva in my mouth.

I watched as she reached out and gently wrapped her right hand around the hilt of the sword. It flared a vibrant blue before settling down. It recognized the Pendragon blood in her. While it didn't revert back to the bracelet form, it wasn't actively trying to skewer the man attempting to save my life.

"That's a new one," J.T. muttered before bending down again. "Let's try this again. Can you tell me your name?"

"M-Morgan," I answered.

"Great. Your pulse is pretty fast right now Morgan. I know this is scary, but I need you to try and take a couple of deep breaths for me."

I inhaled deep through my nose and blew it out as best I could through my mouth. The queasy feeling subsided minimally as I repeated the exercise. He checked my pulse again.

"Good. Just keep breathing like that while I take a look at the wound here."

He donned medical gloves and probed at my stomach, peeling away the blood-soaked fabric of my shirt. He glanced over at the blonde woman. What had he called her?

"Did you see how big the blade was?"

"A couple of inches," Jules answered for her. I watched my friend point to the ambulance. "She needs to go to hospital."

"I'm going to do everything I can to help your friend." He nodded towards Emerys and Excalibur. "I think I have somewhere safer than a hospital that we can take her too. Because I'm guessing none of you want to explain why you're walking around Boston with a magic sword."

The way he threw around the word 'magic,' so casually surprised me.

"You thinking what I think you are?" the other woman said.

"Headquarters. I should be able to handle everything there." He pivoted his attention back to me. "Morgan, I'm sure it's no fun having this thing sticking out of you. But I'm going to need to keep it in there just a little longer, okay?"

"Better to keep it in," I said. "Keeping all my innards where they're supposed to stay."

"Exactly. I'm going to stabilize it for now and then we're going to get you out of here."

Jules squeezed my hand tight as J.T. produced a roll of gauze and began wrapping it around the switchblade. The pain appeared to dissipate as he moved, and I could swear I tasted something sweet on my tongue that overpowered the coppery taste of blood. Then again, for all I knew I was going into shock from being stabbed. Either way, there was little I could do, but lay still while he worked.

"I'm going to need you to help me roll her," he

said, addressing the blonde woman as he produced a backboard.

Awkwardly, they rolled me onto the board and loaded me into the back of the ambulance. It was only then that it occurred to me that someone else would need to drive the vehicle. Medics came in pairs, didn't they? J.T. settled in the back of the rig with me, as did Jules and Emerys. That left the other woman, whose name I still couldn't recall to drive.

"You sure you're qualified for this?" Jules called up to her in the driver's seat as she started the engine.

"Trust me, you'd rather have me up here than back there."

The engine revved and we headed out. The sweetness I'd picked up on before seemed to permeate the back of the ambulance. As it draped over me like a comforting blanket, I was able to identify it as honey.

"You're using magic?" I looked at J.T. for confirmation.

"Just trying to keep you comfortable until we get where we're headed."

It wasn't an outright admission, but it wasn't a denial either. As I studied him—his tussled hair and kind eyes—I was struck with a pang of loss that gripped my chest. His pain stole my breath for a moment. Just long enough for him to notice and press a stethoscope to my chest.

"Could she have suffered other injuries we cannot see?" Emerys still clutched Excalibur tight.

"It's possible," he replied.

"I'm fine," I managed.

"That's debatable," J.T. muttered as he turned in his seat and unhooked an oxygen mask from a contraption on the interior wall of the vehicle. "Just until we get there," he said and slid the mask over my head.

Part of me wanted to protest that I didn't need the extra air. Despite that, it did make breathing easier, and I no longer felt as though I had an elephant sitting on my chest. The ambulance made a sharp turn and J.T.'s hands flew out to steady me, one hand pressed to my side, and the other clamped down on the handle of the knife.

"Sorry," the woman up front called.

As we trundled along, a flurry of questions danced through my mind. Could the blonde woman have been the one I had seen in my dream? And why did so much of this place feel familiar? How had I sensed J.T.'s loss? And what was that all about?

For the time being, there was little chance I

would get answers to any of my questions. The honey-tinged magic that had enveloped me was tugging me toward sleep. I'd slept on the plane, but it wasn't what I'd call restful. Wait, wasn't there some medical concern about repeatedly passing out from an injury like this? Or was that a concussion?

"Hang in there, Morgan. I've got you." J.T.'s voice was soft and the way he spoke carried with it a hint of permission to rest. And so, I slipped into the darkness of unconsciousness again.

WHEN I REGAINED consciousness the second time, I was in far less pain. Something soft and non-moving supported my body. I opened my eyes, finding myself in a small bedroom with blankets tucked up to my chin. I raised my hand to feel a plush pillow beneath my head. Emerys stood sentinel by the window; sword propped against her leg. Jules sat in a chair in the corner slumped over. J.T. and the other woman were absent.

"How long ..." I rasped, drawing Emerys from her reverie.

"A couple of hours."

"Ugh! We've lost nearly eight hours already. Maybe more ..." I groaned.

She was at the bedside in an instant, her hand pressed to my bicep. "You did what you believed was right. You defended someone in need."

"But for all I know it was way off base and I made the wrong choice."

"I watched you, Morgan. You have learned to rely on your magic, and it has not led you astray yet. I trust that we are where we are meant to be." After a beat, she added with a wry, sad smile, "Besides, quests are not meant to be completed so easily."

"Whoever thought quests were a good idea should be shot," I grumbled.

Just then, the door opened and J.T. walked in. He looked paler, the skin around his eyes and mouth a bit drawn as if he'd overexerted himself. "You're looking better," he commented.

"Sorry to say you're not." The words slipped before I could stop them.

He laughed. "Yeah, it took more out of me than I thought to heal your wound. Not my first knife wound, though. Not sure whether to be grateful for that or not." The way he looked down at his hands drew my focus. He spun a simple band around his left ring finger as he spoke. For a split second, an image filled my mind that I had no right to know—J.T. standing with a redheaded woman in a room, pledging their wedding vows. I could swear the woman looked exactly like Ezri.

What had she said to me in the cave? I was coming to her old stomping grounds and there were people I could trust.

"This is going to sound a bit mad, but can I ask you something?"

"Sure."

I pointed to his hand. "Were you married in like a courthouse?"

He stopped fiddling with the band. "What made you ask that?"

"I just saw ... Nevermind. It's probably just the blood loss."

"No, tell me what you saw."

"You getting married to a redheaded woman."

"Morgan, what are you doing?" Emerys pressed tighter on my arm.

"You can't have known that," J.T. said, his voice catching in his throat.

"You're right. I have no way of knowing that. We're strangers, and yet, when I set out on my journey here, a woman told me I'd find people I could trust. And I think maybe that's her way of telling me, you're one of those people."

"What woman?"

"She said her name was Ezri."

J.T.'s face visibly clouded with emotion. His Adam's apple bobbed in his throat as he sunk to a seated position on the edge of the bed. "There is no way you could have talked to Ezri. She—"

"Died," I finished for him. "Yeah, she mentioned that too."

"I mean, there was a time after her death that she came back to say her goodbyes, but that was two years ago."

"She said something about the universe having a way of sorting things out."

"Sounds like her, although she spent a long time hating the universe for what it took from her."

"She seemed pretty chill about the whole thing."

"In the end, I think she accepted what the universe required of her, but for a while she cut herself off from the rest of us. I miss her every day. Our time together wasn't long enough."

"If it makes you feel better, I'm pretty sure I felt her earlier. Before I found your friend being mugged by that knife-wielding prat."

"Sometimes I catch a hint of her power or things that remind me of her."

"Strawberries. Uh, that's what I picked up most."

"The scent of her magic. She had a real knack for picking up on the scent of a person's magic. She could follow it pretty well by the end, too."

It wasn't a skill I'd ever considered, and I certainly wasn't in a position to be able to use it. Was I? I couldn't recall ever being able to sense another person's magic by the scent it gave off before. And yet I'd definitely picked up on the hint of Ezri's power in this city. And J.T.'s magic in the ambulance too. Was this somehow linked to Ezri guiding me?

"Mind telling me where we are?"

J.T. nodded and cleared his throat. "This is Authority headquarters. The Council is a thirteen-member magical governing body that keeps the practice of magic under control and good magic safe."

"So magic isn't openly practiced here?"

"Oh, it is, but we try our best not to let mundane people in on the secret unless we have to. We police our own and teach the younger generations how to harness and use their power."

"Sounds like back in London," I murmured.

"I wouldn't be surprised to know other places have similar set ups. Ezri was on the Council before she died. For a long time, it had been a hereditary thing, but due to some unforeseen circumstances, that changed a few years ago."

I pushed myself into a seated position, grateful that my stomach muscles didn't refuse to cooperate. "I'm sorry I brought all of this up for you. I appreciate you saving my life, though."

"I'm a Healer. It's what I do. Avery did the right thing by calling me."

Avery!

"Today is going to be the day for weird questions, but what is her last name?"

"Fellowes. She married Ezri's cousin Desmond. Why?"

"Is she still here?"

"Probably. Why?"

"Because when I had my, uh, conversation with Ezri, she specifically told me to seek out someone called Avery Fellowes. She thought they might be able to help with a problem we need to fix."

"Morgan, perhaps you should simply rest." Emerys fixed me with a warning glare.

She wasn't quite ready to trust J.T. or Avery with

the reason for our arrival in the States. Still, Ezri had pointed me in this direction. If Emerys trusted that I was leading us towards a way to save Camelot, I was willing to extend a little trust their way.

"We don't have time to rest," I said, throwing off the blankets.

"I would agree with your friend. You just suffered a serious injury. Your body needs time to heal," J.T. urged.

"Funny thing about being the Chosen One, you don't really get the chance to rest. Now, where can I find Avery?"

"I'm right here." The blonde woman stood just outside the room looking as pale as J.T. "I think I know why you're here." She held up a broken gold chain. "That man, he stole my pendant and I think you're supposed to help me get it back."

EIGHT

The relief that flooded my body was enough to sap what little energy I had. I slumped against the doorframe and felt two pairs of hands reach out to steady me. I looked over my shoulder to find Jules on one side and J.T. on the other.

"Come on, Avery can explain while you rest," J.T. pleaded.

"Well, I'm not going to argue with the doctor." Avery stepped into the room and closed the door behind him.

I let J.T. settle me back in the bed and took a few slow breaths. "So, I know why I think I was supposed to find you, but why do you think I'm meant to help you?" I looked at the woman standing at the foot of the bed, her glasses perched on the end of her nose.

"This is going to sound strange, but my husband warned me something like this was coming. That I was meant to be somewhere besides Boston."

"Why's that weird?" Jules pressed.

"Because Des has been dead longer than Ezri," J.T. answered. He fixed Avery with an anxious glance. "How long has this been going on?"

She shrugged. "Not that long. A month or so. It started a little before Thanksgiving. It was like he wanted me to know that it was okay. That I shouldn't feel guilty for leaving the city. I think he just wants me to know I've got a place somewhere out in the world."

"Ezri did mention you were the person to hunt down to fix our particular magical problem," I continued.

It caught the other woman by surprise. "Ezri?"

"Uh, yeah, I sort of had a conversation with her in a magical cave."

"I'm going to need more than that."

"We do not have time for drawn-out explanations." Emerys moved to stand at the head of the bed, Excalibur pressed to her left leg.

I could feel the blade's magic reaching out, as if

making certain I was still nearby. Without thinking, I reached over and wrapped my fingers around the hilt, pressing my palm to the large sapphire. Energy thrummed from the sword up my arm and settled in my core, easing the residual discomfort from being stabbed.

"The short version is we came through a portal from another realm, one that exists alongside this world. While I was there, I had a magical encounter with Ezri, and she told me to find you. She said we'd have allies here," I repeated.

"She's not wrong about the allies part," J.T. admitted.

"Why did she think I could specifically help?" Avery fiddled with the broken part of her necklace.

"She said you're good with magic and technology. We're currently dealing with a magical cyberattack. It took down our kingdom's entire infrastructure. If we don't find a way to undo it in the next four days, we're fucked."

"She means the assholes in the next kingdom over are going to start a war," Jules offered helpfully.

"No pressure there," Avery muttered.

"Do you think you could help them, Avery?" J.T. glanced from her to me and back again.

"Well, I'd have to see the system and ... I'm sorry,

but another realm ... that's going to take me some time to wrap my head around."

"Believe me, I understand. I spent the first three decades of my life here, in this world, in London. But I promise that Camelot is real, and we need all the help we can get."

"If I can, I will help."

"Great. Now, about that necklace. I think you're right that we're meant to help you, too." I prodded the compass still hanging around my neck. "This thing has sent me on a couple of quests now and I think it showed me what looked like your necklace. I don't know why it's so important, though. Last time we went off on one of these, it brought us to the Holy Grail."

"I don't think it's that epic, but it is a family heirloom," Avery answered.

"I've never seen you wear it before," J.T. noted.

For a moment, I wondered just how close the pair were really. They certainly looked like they'd spent a lot of time in each other's orbits. Still, the way Avery rolled her eyes at his words suggested they hadn't been close in a long time.

"I hadn't worn it since I moved to the East Coast. Like I said, it's a family heirloom. But I have been having this recurring dream about it the last couple of weeks and this morning, I decided to put it on. Only now, it's been stolen, and I feel like a piece of me is missing."

"We'll do everything we can to get it back to you." I sat up a little straighter, unsupported. "I'll be honest though; I didn't get that good of a look at it. Is it something that might fetch a lot of money at a pawn shop?"

"It's a single amethyst stone, set in eighteen karat gold. I can't imagine it would be worth that much."

"Is it imbued with magic?" Emerys interjected.

"I ... I don't know. I never asked."

Given what we'd encountered the last time we'd gone off on a quest, my gut told me that Avery's pendant had some sort of magical affinity. But as I lay back on the pillows, a realization crashed down upon me. We were in an unfamiliar city looking for a thief none of us knew. Did they have magical police here? Surely, we weren't meant to just rely on mundane authorities for this.

"Anyone have a suggestion on where we start looking?"

"Well, I could reach out to some contacts to see about accessing the video cameras in the area. See if we could at least get a good still image of the guy," Avery said.

"Why do I get the feeling this wouldn't be legal?"

"Well, it's not strictly illegal, but it would definitely be off-the-book." She grinned. "Sometimes it pays to know law enforcement."

"Are they someone we can trust?"

"There's no one I would trust more." Avery pulled out her phone. "Let me make a call. You should sleep a little more. Something tells me you're going to need your strength."

Except I didn't want to sleep. It would mean losing precious time in getting back to Camelot before all hell broke loose. And yet, a sudden wave of exhaustion cascaded over me, and I couldn't help but nestle back against the pillows. My right hand still held Excalibur and as I started to slip into slumber, I almost expected Emerys to relieve me of the blade. Instead, she lifted it up and laid the sword across my torso. Sleepily I pressed my right index finger to the gem in the hilt and the sword transformed back into a bracelet, settling safely around my left wrist.

THE SUNLIGHT HAD DIMMED when I woke again. This time, the unease at being in an unfamiliar place vanished when I opened my eyes. The room was cast in shadows, but it was almost peaceful. The chair where Julayne had been dozing earlier sat empty. Emerys remained at the window.

"You know you don't have to watch over me like I'm a child," I pointed out and sat up, feeling more refreshed.

"We are in a strange place, and I am worried for your safety." Her brow creased. "I did not expect you to throw yourself head-first into the path of oncoming harm so easily."

"Guess I'm learning to be a hero. Isn't that what I'm supposed to do?" After a moment of silence, I added, "Besides, it's not like you batted an eye when I was getting tossed around like a rag doll during the tournament a few months back."

"Forgive an old woman for worrying over the safety of her kin," she murmured.

I wanted to point out that she didn't look the part of an old woman in the least. But I could appreciate her concern. We were blood after all. It still felt weird to *have* kin let alone think that without her, I wouldn't have existed. "Look, I'm bound to get into scrapes. We just have to trust that I'm going to bounce back from it."

I didn't want to think about the alternative. I gestured to the empty chair. "Where's Jules?"

"She went to see about some food with your healer friend."

On cue, my stomach rumbled. I couldn't recall the last time I'd eaten. Kicking the blankets off, I stood and stretched. My body didn't feel sore or incumbered by the recent trauma anymore. I took it as a good sign and started for the door. "Morgan, I am sorry if you feel I have treated you as if you are not capable of protecting yourself."

"It's fine. You spent just as long worrying you'd never find me as I did thinking I'd never amount to anything. Both of us still need to adjust. Now come on, Jules had the right idea about food."

In hindsight, I shouldn't have just marched off as if I knew where a bloody thing was located. I'd entered this place unconscious and easily wound up in a closet before long. I backed out and eased the door shut, moving down the hall until I found a set of winding stairs. It looked promising and I descended to find the first floor with several rooms off either side of the staircase. Portraits adorned the walls, and I spotted one of Ezri. It was less a portrait and more a simple framed photograph, but it stood out amongst the rest.

"She was so very young," Emerys said in my ear. She reached out her hand and traced the tip of her index finger along the woman's jawline. "She almost looks like ... " She trailed off as a door to our right opened and Jules materialized.

"Good, you're up. Come on, we've got food."

I followed my friend, leaving Emerys to stare at Ezri's photo. I found J.T. seated, in what appeared to be an industrial kitchen, at a long table with platters of sandwiches laid out. A pitcher of water sat next to the food, and I picked up on the scent of coffee beans percolating. I eyed the machine sitting on the counter, some empty mugs beside it, and made a stop to fill up on caffeine.

"Avery have any luck with her mysterious contacts?" I set the mug down and slid onto one of the benches attached to the table.

"She left about an hour ago and isn't back yet," J.T. replied, pushing a tray toward me. "You should eat."

I snickered. "Why do I get the feeling you've done this before?"

"Because my wife was nothing if not laser-focused when she was on a case. Things like eating and taking care of herself tended to be the first things to go."

"Sounds like she and I have a lot in common."

"I'm starting to see that."

I took a bite of a ham and Swiss sandwich with a hint of mustard and studied the man across from me. "I wanted to apologize again for just dropping into your life and bringing up your wife."

"It's fine. Really." His cheeks flushed. "But, if I'm being honest, I had actually gone a few months without her filling my every thought."

"You really must have loved her," Jules said.

"I did. Even when she cut me off for a decade, I never lost hope that we'd find our way back to each other. And we did. For nine months we were happy. And then the universe demanded her life to restore balance. And the rest of us were left behind to pick up the pieces."

"Magic's a bitch," I declared after picking up a second sandwich.

"Sometimes I would agree with you on that," he sighed just as the kitchen door opened and Avery appeared. Despite the circumstances under which we found ourselves, she looked pleased.

"Oh good, you're up. How are you feeling?"

I raised the partially eaten sandwich at her. "Better. Thanks. Any luck on your end?"

"I managed to convince an old friend to give me access to the footage. We should have it within the hour."

"And what about finding the prat once you get a good image?" Jules pressed. "I mean, don't you need facial recognition or something for that? No offense, but you don't look like you'd be able to magic that one out of thin air."

"You're not wrong. I can't just pull it out of my ass. Luckily that same friend is giving us a small window to use their database for anything we need to find." She retrieved a coffee cup from beside the coffee pot and filled it, coming to sit beside me. "Not that I haven't found ways to get into those types of databases without help."

"You're more of a grey hat, eh?" I couldn't hide the surprise in my tone.

"Yeah. I mean I've been more legit since Ezri. But sometimes a girl's gotta get a little creative to solve problems."

"I'm not saying you aren't going to be able to find this guy, but I don't see how that's supposed to fix our problem," Jules noted.

"Jules, don't be such a bitch," I chided.

"No, she has a point. Everything I'm doing now is just tech skills. Honestly, I'm not sure how I'm going to help you back in your home. But I can tell you that I've used magic to manipulate data and videos to uncover dark magic. If there's anything like that keeping you cut off, I'll find it."

"Well, let's just hope that whatever we're up against is something you can solve," I said.

The room grew quiet save for the sounds of chewing and the occasional clank of cups on the table. It felt almost like we were back in Camelot, sharing a meal with members of the Council. I could almost picture Shunae seated beside J.T. I wouldn't exactly call us friends, but she'd proven to be someone I could count on. At the very least, I knew she had Camelot's best interest in mind. And she'd worked tirelessly to secure what should have been peace with Uther and his people. Anyone who had the balls to sit in a room with that bastard and not throttle him, deserved my respect.

As I downed the last of my coffee, I watched as J.T. stood and left the room. I tracked his movement with my eyes before turning my focus on the women still in the room with me. Much like I could picture Shunae seated here with us, I could see Avery at the table in the castle, looking right at home. Maybe that's why we'd been led to her. I knew I was going to need allies in the coming fight against Arthur and his father. I'd seen as much in the Crystal Cave. Maybe Avery was destined to be one of those at my side.

"I'd say you're going to owe me for this, but I think it's time that I do you some favors," a dark-skinned woman with a tight bun at the nape of her neck said, filling the doorway.

Somehow, I could tell she wasn't magical in the slightest. And yet, her presence exuded so much power I couldn't help but give her my attention.

"Morgan, meet Special Agent Jacquie DeWitt," Avery introduced. "She's not a witch, but she's the next best thing."

NINE

Agent DeWitt stayed where she stood, blocking the doorway as she appraised the rest of our contingent. It was then that I realized Emerys was still missing in action. Jules arched a dark brow. "You know coppers?"

"Careful Jules, you actually sound impressed," I teased, nudging her shoulder.

"You didn't tell me we had overseas company," Agent DeWitt said as she finally moved closer to where we sat. I couldn't explain how or why, but I got the sense she expected someone else to be there. She held out her hand expectantly. "You are?"

"Morgan le Fey." I gripped her out-stretched hand in a firm handshake.

"Crown Princess," Jules added, making me cringe.

Technically true, but I still couldn't get used to hearing it aloud. Thank God most of the time there wasn't a need for such formalities within Camelot's castle walls.

"Royalty?" Agent DeWitt gave me an approving nod.

"It's complicated," I muttered and pulled my hand back. I cleared my throat, "And this is my best mate, Jules."

In short order, they exchanged pleasantries and Agent DeWitt looked at Avery. "Your message said something about you being robbed. That's why you needed me to pull the footage."

"Yeah. It seems like Morgan and her friends are here on a mission of sorts too," Avery began.

"Quest really," Jules corrected.

"Whatever you want to call it. They're looking for someone to help them protect their home and I think I'm meant to be that person. First though, they're going to help me get my family heirloom back."

I wanted to explain that I had a hunch her pendant was more than a mere family relic. The chalice—or grail—had been extremely valuable because of its magical lineage. But without seeing the pendant up close in person, I couldn't be sure.

"And what led you to this conclusion?" Agent DeWitt continued, her tone taking on the cadence of a practiced interrogator.

"Ezri," Avery answered simply.

The other woman's expression shifted immediately. Changing to a look of sad resignation—similar to the one I'd seen on J.T.'s face when I first brought up my dearly departed tour guide. I stood, the plate on the table clattering loud enough to draw the focus to myself. "Not that I'm ungrateful for her assistance, but is literally everyone in this bloody city linked to this woman?"

Agent DeWitt cast a disapproving glare my way. "How do you know my partner?"

I blinked. "Partner?"

"Before I joined the FBI, Ezri was my partner on the Boston police force."

"I'd say that's a yes to your question, Morgan," Jules stage whispered.

"Her ghost appeared to Morgan in a cave or something and sent her on this quest." J.T.'s voice came from behind Agent DeWitt.

"I see." Silence fell over the kitchen while she processed the information. Finally, she produced a small computer drive and passed it to Avery. "This is what I could pull in the area. Work your magic."

"It must be such a strange thing, to be so rooted to this world and not able to fully partake." Emerys' re-appearance made me jump. I pivoted to see her addressing the agent.

"That's one way of putting it. But I don't see how people like Ezri could do what she needed to do, not without the rest of us mundane folks to give her the cover she needed."

"I regret I didn't have a chance to meet her." The way Emerys moved through the space in a daze was unnerving. The tiny hairs on the nape of my neck bristled in warning. This was not the woman who'd banished two sword-wielding Seelie assassins from my flat with a wave of her hand.

"Now that we have the footage, we should see if we can find out where the asshole went," Avery announced. "You said you were on a clock."

I set my empty coffee cup in the industrial sink, along with the plate and followed Avery out of the space and back upstairs. Instead of heading for the area where I'd convalesced, she marched straight to a set of double doors. She threw them open without losing a step. Thirteen chairs sat in a semi-circle in the middle of the room. The weight of the magic that had come through this space was palpable, pressing against my body with its own mass.

"This is the Council meeting room," she explained before taking a right through a doorway and heading down a short corridor to a smaller room with computer screens and keyboards. "And this is where I work."

"Bit hidden away, isn't it?" I remarked.

She shrugged as she plugged the drive in with a cord sitting on the desk and fiddled with the mouse. "Honestly, for a lot of my life I've felt more comfortable like this. I'm good with computers. I understand them. People aren't always my strong suit." A wistful look passed over her pale features. "Des would always say that he brought me out of my shell."

"He'd be proud you didn't retreat after everything happened," Agent DeWitt said from the doorway behind me.

Jules, J.T., and Emerys remained in the Council Chamber. As it was, there was barely enough space for the three of us. I focused my attention on the screen that lit up as Avery accessed the FBI drive. I spotted the footage labeled as BPD. It would seem Agent DeWitt still had sway in her old department. Interesting.

"You ready for this?" Avery looked at me over the tops of her glasses.

For a split second I couldn't understand why she was concerned whether I was ready to watch her being mugged. Then phantom pains danced through my stomach muscles, and I swallowed a lump in my throat. "Uh, yeah. Play it."

If Agent DeWitt's curiosity piqued at our exchange, she didn't telegraph it. She stood silent and stoic on Avery's other side as the blonde woman hit 'Play.' A large expanse of the park where we'd found Avery appeared on the screen. People walked by going about their lives, unaware of the violence about to erupt in their midst. I spotted myself, Jules, and Emerys moving into frame just as the assailant approached Avery. He grabbed her and I saw myself intervene. Somehow, I'd missed him snag the pendant off the chain before I tackled him to the ground. I winced as his knife found its way into my stomach.

For his part, the mugger looked surprised I'd actually gotten in the way of his blade. In the following chaos, he scrambled to his feet and took off, mask disappearing into his pocket. I blinked and he was gone. My eyes tracked the Common around me as the other women crowded in, using their phones to call in reinforcements. But as my mind processed what I'd seen, I realized something didn't add up. Where did he go? There wasn't a crowd he could slip away into.

"Something's wrong," I blurted unhelpfully.

"He pulled a disappearing act. Not the first time we've seen that," Agent DeWitt replied. Out of the corner of my eye, I caught her retrieve her phone.

"Hold off on calling Kayla," Avery said, as if sensing Agent DeWitt's intent. "Like she's told us before, they don't all know each other. Let's see what I might be able to do to clear this up. Give me a minute."

I watched as she reached out her hand and pressed her fingertips to the screen. The image flickered, rewinding almost of its own volition to the point where my attacker was on his feet, but had not yet vanished. Avery's brow furrowed a bit as the images passed frame by frame at half speed. It appeared almost as if the man glitched with each step he took. I tracked his every stuttering movement away from us until he vanished pixel by pixel.

"Yeah, I don't think that made it better," I noted.

"Sometimes you have to get inside the tech to really see what's going on," Avery answered, breaking contact with the monitor.

I had no idea what the bloody hell that even meant. "We're not about to jump into some weird Matrix-level shit, are we?"

She smiled to herself. "I suppose in a way we are. Or I am anyway."

"Whatever you plan on doing, I want in."

She pivoted in her chair to look me directly in the eye. "No offense, but I work better with people whose magic I know as well as my own. This is delicate work."

"And that fucker tried to kill me."

"Her Highness has a point," Agent DeWitt snickered.

"Fine, I get it, okay, but you have to do whatever I tell you. And try to remember that what we're seeing has already happened. We can't change anything."

"Got it."

She held out her right hand and I took it in my left. As she reached back toward the computer monitor, I felt the sapphire at the heart of the bracelet warm against my skin. My magic came unbidden to mind, ready to wash over everything. It was a feeling I hadn't had since my initial arrival in Camelot and certainly not one I'd ever experienced in this world. It sent a shiver of nerves through my body.

Before I could voice my concern, the tiny computer room vanished, replaced by the park scene we'd been watching in slow motion. I wasn't certain whether I could safely let go of Avery's hand, so I waited for her to break contact first. If she was comfortable moving independently then there was a good chance it wouldn't result in anything catastrophic happening.

"This is sort of like reliving a memory," I commented mostly to myself.

"Yeah, just it's the computer's memory. Come on. He went this way."

She took off away from the scene where I lay bleeding out on the pavement, and I was grateful that we weren't focused on my injury. It wasn't that I couldn't handle the sight of blood. I'd gotten through life so far not having to witness my own bodily injury and I wasn't sure I wouldn't see Nim's body superimposed over mine. The wounds were eerily similar.

"So, how exactly would this prick be able to just vanish?" I asked. The scenery around us shifted as the video footage played on, still at half speed.

"Magic," Avery deadpanned.

"Obviously."

"Some people are really good at hiding in plain sight. Sometimes that comes back to bite them in the ass though. The number of people who its happened to is bigger than you might expect. They call themselves Whisperers."

"Sometimes turning invisible sounds like a nice existence."

"I've got a friend who would disagree." She pointed ahead of us. "There."

The video resumed playing full speed. We watched our mugger and would-be killer shimmer and turn incorporeal. I reached out a hand and magic flooded my nerve endings. Without intending it, I'd dismantled his spell, and he stood there mid-motion, his back toward us.

"Okay, that's neat." Avery sounded genuinely impressed.

"Sometimes my magic is a bit overzealous."

"No, this is good. We can get a better image for facial recognition. We should have a really good shot at finding this guy now."

"You realize he's probably pawned the pendant by now," I pointed out as she waved her hands in front of the man's face, as if capturing his image on a tablet or phone.

"Knowing who he is, will tell us where he might have gone. And there's only so many places you can fence stolen objects, magical or otherwise in this city."

That assumed he stayed local. I didn't voice my doubts since it wouldn't have been helpful. Avery gave a satisfied nod and returned to my side. She held her hand, palm up and waggled her fingers in a 'hold on' gesture. I did as she indicated, and the video surroundings popped out of view. Once again, we were in the tiny room off the Council meeting chamber. My vision swam at the sudden shift in orientation, and I gripped the edge of the desk in front of me.

Beside me, I heard Avery's fingers moving over the keyboard. I was only vaguely aware of what she was doing as she tapped away. Images flew past rapid-fire on the screen. Once my head stopped spinning, I realized she'd somehow managed to actually bring back the clear image of the man's face from our deep dive inside the video. Facial recognition finally produced a hit.

"Leyton Danson," she said, reading aloud from what turned out to be an arrest record for petty theft.

At least he was consistent.

"His name doesn't sound familiar from my current circles," Jacquie said from the doorway. "But that doesn't mean he hasn't crossed paths with people who would have reason to want a magical object."

"His name doesn't ring any bells for me either, but I want to check one other thing." Avery's fingers went rat-a-tat-tat on the keyboard again and a directory appeared on screen.

She entered his name and waited for the search to populate results. She frowned and pushed her glasses up the bridge of her nose. "Well, he's not specifically listed in the Authority's database, but we do have someone with the same last name."

"We might not know where he could have pawned the pendant, but that stuff would tell you if he's got a job, right?" I leaned over, pointing at the edge of his police mug shot.

"I mean, technically it would be in his police file. This is just surface stuff though. Things you could find with a creative civilian search."

Fabric rustled and Agent DeWitt stepped up, making a shooing gesture. Avery spun in the chair, averting her gaze. I was a little slower on the uptake as Agent DeWitt entered her credentials, paving the way for the deeper dive we needed to determine where our search for Leyton Danson would lead next.

"I saw nothing," Avery professed as she turned around, studying the newly revealed information. A moment later, her features brightened. "We're in luck. He's got a job at Notre Dame."

"Come again?"

"I'll explain on the way. Come on."

"You're on your own for this part. I don't want any part of whatever happens next," Agent DeWitt said, stepping out of our away.

Her words filled me with unease as Avery led the way from the computer room and back into the more spacious Council Chamber. J.T. had left in the intervening time. Emerys and Jules waited in two of the chairs on the outer edges of the semi-circle of chairs.

"Where's J.T.?"

"His employer required his assistance for an additional shift," Emerys answered. She still had that dazed look. Now wasn't the time to press her about the change in her demeanor. We had more pressing matters to attend.

"Please tell me you've found something." Jules sounded irritated.

"Apparently, we're going to some place called Notre Dame."

TEN

Afternoon had faded into evening by the time we made our way into the bustling college hub of the city. I'd been so out of it during the ambulance ride, I hadn't been aware of how far we'd traveled. However, it had taken a solid twenty-five minutes to get from our starting point to our apparent destination through traffic. I marveled at how similar the club scene pace was to London nightlife, even down to the young women in ridiculously short skirts and leggings.

"Brings back memories, eh?" Jules noted with a chuckle.

"Oh, come on, our clientele was way posher than this," I countered.

Avery arched a brow at us, and I smiled. "Tended bar back home in London."

"Then you're going to fit right in."

We moved along the sidewalk in a small cluster. I took in the hazy streetlights overhead and managed to hide the fact the loud screeching of a train speeding by behind us hadn't made me nearly jump out of my skin. I needed to not give off 'tourist' vibes right now. I knew what that did to the London locals and I could only imagine Boston was the same. Avery stopped walking and gestured to a sign overhead that read, 'Notre Dame.' The line of would-be patrons waiting to get inside snaked down the street and around the corner of an adjacent building out of sight. The Witching Hour never had lines this long.

"What do they serve here, magic-infused booze?"

"You know, I've never asked, but part of me wouldn't be surprised."

I didn't envy the crowd waiting to get in. The November air had chilled with the sun well sunk past the horizon and I shivered. But we also didn't have time to play nice and wait our turn to get inside. If Leyton worked here, the window to catch him off guard would be shrinking with every minute we wasted.

"Any thoughts on how we're going to get in?"

"That's easy," Avery said as she marched right up to the beefy looking bouncer. I couldn't sense any magic coming from him, but the fact he stood out in this weather in short sleeves with no hint of chill suggested something otherworldly was going on. Avery whispered something to the man and his gaze slid over me, then Jules and Emerys.

"I'd say you're running low on the boss' good will, but I think he actually kind of likes you," he noted in a deep bass as we cut the line.

Music thrummed in my breastbone the moment the door shut behind us. We were in a small dark entryway that led into a larger interior. Bass beats pulsed with every step, and I could feel a headache threatening to settle behind my eyes the longer we were in here. Fuck, I hated techno music.

The pressure on my head only grew once we stepped into the bar proper. There was an open space in the center for a dance floor, with high-top tables spread out around it. A high wooden bar ran the length of the wall nearest us, and I spotted a handful of patrons dotting the length of it. My vision blurred as the pain in my head did a crescendo in time with the music. The scent of lime coated my tongue and my skin felt almost sticky with it as my magic rose up to try and relieve the discomfort.

Take the pain away.

The magic obeyed in an instant and my vision cleared. It allowed me to take stock of the set-up behind the bar. It wasn't the worst layout I'd seen in a place like this, but it wasn't how I'd have laid things out. My fingers twitched at the thought of slipping behind the bar and reordering things.

"She's not here," a handsome man said from down the other end of the bar.

I hadn't realized I'd been staring at him until he spoke. I could almost see the bulk of something more around his shoulders and torso as he moved to sling a towel over one shoulder. Avery closed the distance, clearly comfortable with the man. I hung back a pace or two to assess him.

"Good thing that isn't who I'm here to see," Avery said over the din of the bar's cacophony.

The man leaned his thick forearms on the bar. "What sort of shady shit are you bringing into my bar now?"

"You're really going to let him talk to you like that?" The words left my mouth—full of righteous indignation and fire—before I'd even registered the thought.

"Who the hell are you?" His Boston accent was thick as he glared at me.

"Morgan le Fey. Who the fuck are you?" I countered.

"The owner of this establishment and if you keep mouthing off, I'll be the one throwing your ass out."

"Okay, why don't we all just calm down?" Avery's tone was conciliatory even though her face betrayed clear unease at the situation. The skin around her eyes and lips puckered, and worry lines wrinkled the skin above her nose. "We're here looking for one of your employees. So, if there is shady shit going on, it's on them, not us."

The bartender looked skeptical in the dim light. "What employee?"

"Leyton Danson. His police file said he works here," I filled in.

"Worked, past tense. Fired that kid weeks ago. Couldn't show up on time and had the memory of a damn goldfish."

"So, we just wasted all that time for nothing," I railed.

Power flooded me as my emotions escalated.

Unlike when we'd returned to London in search of the chalice, this quest for lack of a better term felt more consequential. My entire kingdom—people who would one day count on me—was at risk. Magic coalesced around me like a protective shell, hardening into a translucent barrier. I felt the electrical currents in the air from the lighting and the sound systems bumping against my spell and sparks flew, cascading down around people's heads. Out of nowhere, I spotted something glowing on the rafters overhead. My spell cracked before it shattered, and I fell to my knees.

Emerys was at my side in an instant, one hand pressed against my back for support, the other hand reaching to pull me onto my feet again. *What the hell was that?* I looked across the space at the bartender, whose gaze had drifted upward for a moment.

"Nice to know those are working again."

"You always treat your guests like criminals?" I spat as my body finally regained equilibrium.

"Look lady, I've had enough shit go down in this bar that I'm not taking any more chances. Now, keep your power in check or get the hell out of my bar."

"How about we all just take a breath and calm down?" Avery said, her tone still conciliatory, if a bit high-pitched. "We aren't trying to do damage to your bar. We really are just looking for information."

"And I told you, I fired that punk."

"Perhaps there is other information you might know about him, besides his lack of punctuality, which could assist us in locating him?" When Emerys spoke, her words cut through the din and background noise of the bar.

"There's not much to tell. He was lazy, so I got rid of him."

"How'd you find him in the first place?" I asked, leaning on the edge of the bar. "You don't seem the type of bloke to just hire anyone off the street." I waved my hand around. "Not in a place like this."

"What would you know about hiring in a *place like this*?"

"Back home in London, I basically am you." I didn't add that I wasn't the owner of The Witching Hour. It didn't feel important, or maybe I just needed the ego boost in front of this smarmy prick.

He arched a brow at me, signaling he didn't believe me. My fingers itched to get behind the bar and prove it to him. I felt a firm hand on my wrist and glanced to my left to see Jules giving me a pointed look. Her icy blue eyes flicked to the man across the bar. "As much as I'd love to see Morgan wipe the floor with you, we really don't have time for a pissing contest. Just tell us how Leyton came into your employ, and we'll be out of your hair."

He glared at us and for a brief moment I could feel the magic around us slip. It was as though he was keeping up some sort of illusion, not that I had any idea why. The jewel at the heart of my bracelet thrummed against my pulse point, and in an instant, I knew what Excalibur wanted me to do. It longed to undo whatever spell he was working and reveal the truth.

Not right now.

I didn't like or trust this man, but it did seem bad form to tear down his spells in his own establishment. And for all I knew he had a perfectly good reason for keeping them up. He rubbed at his jaw as he considered the request.

"He was recommended by one of the other servers, Serena. I think they might have dated in the past."

"Where can we find her?"

He pointed across the bar to a wiry brunette in a tight t-shirt and jeans. She was handing out bottles of beer to a small cluster of what looked like college guys. One made a grab for her ass. The same sensation I'd felt when the symbols overhead had knocked me down, danced along my forearms. I could almost make out a tiny strand of magic worming its way across the space in midair to keep his hand off the girl's backside. No doubt he'd think it was just a drunken miss. From behind the bar, Jonathan gave me a grunt. I turned back and spotted a different set of symbols alight in the rafters.

"People like you aren't the only ones I'm warding against."

Maybe I didn't detest him quite as much now.

Jonathan let out a whistle and Serena's head whipped around, making eye contact with him. She marched over and set her empty tray down on the bar. She acted like she didn't see our quartet standing half a foot away.

"He missed," she said, assuming he wanted to talk about the prat with the grabby hands.

"I made sure he did. No one gets away with shit like that in my bar."

She gave him a genuine smile. "One of the reasons I like working here."

He nodded in our direction. "They've got some questions for you about Leyton."

Color drained her cheeks. "I thought you said you fired him."

"I did. But you knew him better than most

everyone. How about you take a break, answer a few questions?"

"I already took my break."

He waved her off. "I'll cover it. Call it hazard pay."

She glanced in our direction again, her eyes settling on Avery and the tension eased from her shoulders a degree. The familiar face seemed to work in our favor. Serena disappeared for a moment, returning a minute later with a jacket. She motioned for us to follow her out the back.

We ended up in a back alley that ran parallel to the street we'd entered on. It wasn't that unlike the layout behind the Witching Hour. I never thought I'd be nostalgic for the place. Yet, in that moment, I missed the familiarity, and the routine. Serena tugged her jacket closer around her torso.

"What do you want to know?"

"You said you and Leyton weren't together anymore. What happened?" Avery looked all business.

Serena shrugged. "People break up. I mean, he wasn't the brightest bulb in the pack, if you know what I mean. He had a penchant for taking advice from the wrong people. Getting involved in things he shouldn't."

"We know he's been arrested before," I offered.

"He'd been doing better about that since we met. But the last few weeks before Jonathan canned him, he'd been acting kind of off."

"Off how?" Avery pushed her glasses up the bridge of her nose.

"If I didn't know better, I'd say he was cheating on me, but he was not that clever. But he'd mentioned something about some new guys he'd been hanging with."

"What sort of guys?" I took a step closer and to her credit, Serena didn't back down.

"I don't know. He was kind of into online gaming. Like multi-player stuff. It wasn't really my thing, so I never asked too many questions. But it could have been there. I just know that once he started hanging with this new crowd, he got secretive."

Avery's demeanor shifted and a hardness came over her features. "You didn't happen to notice if he'd gotten any new tattoos recently?"

"Leyton? No way. He's terrified of needles. He'd never get one."

"You're sure?"

"Dead sure. Not even on a dare."

"Do you know if the address in his police record is current?"

"Yeah. We never lived together or anything."

The image of Leyton vanishing into thin air on the surveillance footage flashed before me. "This might sound a bit mad, but could he do things like ..."

"What, magic?"

My mouth hung open a little. "Yeah."

"Yeah. You don't get hired in a place like this without being in the know. He wasn't great at it, but he could do magic."

"Did he ever just want to disappear?" Avery pressed.

Serena shook her head. "I know what you're asking. But no, it hadn't turned on him. Horrible as it sounds, he wasn't strong willed enough to let it do that to him."

"Thanks. You've been really helpful."

Avery pivoted on her heel and marched around the outside of the building, leaving Jules, Emerys, and I no choice but to follow. Serena ducked back inside, and I waited for the rear exit to close with a slam before I spoke.

"What was with the tattoo question?"

"For a while, we had a bad group operating out of the city and they, uh ... branded their members."

"You talk as if they no longer exist," Emerys pointed out as we emerged back on the main thoroughfare.

"They don't. Or at least they haven't. There was a thing a few months ago where some low-level players tried to make a comeback, but they didn't get very far."

"But you think something similar might be happening now?" I moved to block her path forward.

"Maybe. And moving online would be a smart way to do it."

"Even if that is true, why take your pendant? What's so special about it?"

She shook her head. "That's the thing. I don't know." Worry lines creased her forehead. "But I think I might know where we should look to find out."

ELEVEN

A very took us back to her flat, her energy far surpassing mine. I could tell my companions were also flagging. We needed answers, but we weren't going to be worth a damn without rest.

"I think we should get some sleep," I announced as Avery eased the front door shut.

"Haven't you been telling me that time is of the essence?" she countered.

"Yeah, but we're all still exhausted. And we'll be in far better shape to find Leyton with a few hours' rest, don't you think?"

The brightness in her eyes faded a touch. "I know you're right. I just feel like for the first time in a while, my help's been important, crucial to solving the problem and I don't want to mess it up."

"What do you mean?"

"I moved out here, because I wanted to do something good with my life. I didn't feel like I could accomplish what I was meant to back home. It felt too small. I know that probably sounds stupid."

"Where we are born is not always where we are meant to be," Emerys said.

"Anyway, I came here, and I met Des and everyone. For a while I thought I had a purpose working as a consultant for the police and the FBI. But it never felt quite fulfilling enough. Sure, I found the things they needed and used my skills like that, but I wasn't the one making the real difference. That was the people with the badges and guns, and stronger magic swooping in to save the day."

"You've got a bit of a sidekick complex," Jules said. "Happens to the best of us. Especially those of us not born with a destiny written in the stars."

"I guess so. But with this, it feels like I'm meant to be more than just a side player."

"Getting some sleep and coming back fresh does not mean you will be any less crucial to our endeavor," Emerys assured her. "We would not be here without you after all."

"You guys are welcome to the couch. And I have

a pull-out bed in the office. I'm going to stay up a little longer and see if I can find anything useful."

"Make sure you get some rest, too." I patted her shoulder as I made my way in the direction of what I assumed was the office.

True to her word, there was a small camp bed stowed in a closet. It was tiny, but it would do for a few hours' rest. I turned to find Emerys standing behind me in the doorway. I took in the slump of her posture and the lack of color in her cheeks.

"What's going on with you?" I pointed to the bed and didn't move.

She studied me for a moment before letting out an audible sigh and sinking onto the thin mattress. I moved to lean against the wall, waiting for her to explain what had made her so distracted and out of sorts. Seeing the woman who'd been so strong and fierce upon our first meeting look so worn out was unnerving.

"I hate to admit it, but I believe I am a bit homesick."

"For Camelot?"

"For my ancestral home."

"What's brought this on? You weren't like this when we were in London."

She smoothed the fabric of her shirt and didn't

meet my gaze. "While you convalesced, I spoke with our healer friend."

"About?" I prodded.

"It would seem there is a deeper bond tethering you and the woman who appeared to you in the cave."

"Look, it's late. I'm tired. You're tired. Can you just cut the cryptic shit?"

"I never told you, but not long before I left my home and passed through the gate into Albion, I nearly lost kin. There had been tension amongst our band of druids and one that had broken away who was prone to chaos and darkness. My cousin, Aoife had sought peace with their leader. We were meant to meet where the gate connects this realm to Albion for a truce. But when we arrived, their leader was dead. He'd been slaughtered by his second in command."

"Brutal, but I still don't see the point."

"Some might say it was a miracle any of us walked away that day. But in truth, it was Aoife's doing. She was nearly slain and then she pooled our collective magic to heal herself and grant her more power. She won the day. I did not know then that her bloodline would go on to bear a hero destined to die for this world ... a Savior."

Ezri.

The pieces clicked into place a minute later. "Oh — oh shit. She's like a distant relative."

Emerys nodded slowly. "It is why I believe she came to you in the cave, to guide you."

"It wasn't just because we were coming to her city."

"It was blood calling to blood." She waved a hand around her. "J.T. told me that he and their council believe when she sacrificed herself for them all in the end, she cast protection over this place. This city's magic is woven with her magic like a shield."

I'd sensed Ezri was powerful when we'd met, but to cast a spell so powerful as to linger in the world years later. The notion made me shiver. "So, you've been missing your family. The one you left behind."

"I do not know if I would have been granted such a long life if I had stayed. I doubt I would have known this young woman in her time. Yet I can't help but wonder what it would have been like to see Aoife's line grow and change. If I had been there, would the world have demanded such a steep sacrifice of her descendants?"

"I can't pretend to understand what makes the

universe go round, but I have to believe you were where you were meant to be." I pushed away from the wall and knelt before her, taking her hands in mine. "Besides, if you'd stayed, I'd have never been born. And who knows what sort of chaos Uther and his assholes would be wreaking right now."

That brought a wan smile to her lips. "That is true."

"Come on. Why don't you have a lie down in here? I'll go fight Jules for the couch."

She let one of my hands go and cupped my cheek. "You may not know it, but sometimes you remind me so much of your mother."

"I don't know about that. I'll see you in a few hours."

I left her in the office and retraced my steps back to the small living room. Jules had already settled on the floor under a blanket with a couple of throw pillows. She snored softly when I tiptoed past her. The door to the bedroom sat ajar and I could see a sliver of light peeking through. The sound of someone rummaging through boxes filtered out of the room, but I stayed put. Avery was a big girl, and she could handle being sleep deprived or not.

I TOSSED and turned for the next few hours, drifting in and out of a light doze. Murky images of people in peasant garb filled my dreams. They were faceless and nameless. In my half-awake state, I couldn't make sense of them. The location looked familiar—almost like my brain was taking me back to the barrier between realms. When I finally sat up, hair matted to my forehead in a cold sweat, sunlight shone through the window in thick bands across the floor. Jules no longer occupied the floor and the door to the bedroom was firmly closed.

Wiping the grit from my eyes and hastily pulling my hair into a messy bun at the nape of my neck, I went in search of the loo and noticed the office empty. It wasn't difficult to find and mercifully it was free. That did beg the question where had Emerys and Jules gone. For a split second as I stood washing my hands, I feared someone had kidnapped them in the brief time I'd managed to sleep.

"Who's hungry?" Jules called from the direction of the front door.

I stuck my head out of the bathroom to find her and Emerys coming back inside laden with boxes of donuts and a carry-out box of coffee. I gave her a quizzical look as I moved into the small living space and relieved her of one of the boxes. "You just vanished. I don't like you two just disappearing on me."

"We did not travel far. Julayne didn't think it wise," Emerys explained.

"And I wasn't the one who put a tether spell on us, so that we wouldn't get lost," Jules said with a bemused look.

"We are in an unfamiliar place. I thought it best we didn't get separated if we could help it."

"At least we haven't been arrested yet," I said and opened one of the boxes, taking out a glazed confection.

"Do I want to know?" Avery appeared from the bedroom. She'd changed clothes and looked as if she'd actually gotten some rest.

"Oh, we were basically stealing from the ruins of an old church. Some assholes showed up and tried to stop us. We didn't quite get away in time though," I explained around a bite of donut.

"Yeah, there's definitely more to that story," Avery said and went in search of coffee mugs.

"Well, we *could* tell her about the dragons," Jules said in a conspiratorial tone.

Avery reappeared, coffee mugs hanging off four of her fingers. "I'm sorry, *dragons*?"

"Albion, where I'm, uh, originally from. It's

home to more than just humans. There's fae and dragons, too. We were on the hunt for a magical object that had been brought over to your world by some dragons and happened to run into them." I relieved her of two of the mugs and passed them to Jules and Emerys before taking a third and pouring coffee from the box set on a table in the living room.

"Sorry, I'm just having trouble wrapping my head around this. Dragons are huge. How would we not see them?" She began to pace, empty mug still swinging from her index finger. "Unless they could camouflage themselves. But still, we'd have picked up on something like that right?"

"They can turn human," I explained.

"That ... weirdly makes more sense."

"Morgan's on quite good terms with the royal dragons," Jules drawled.

"Oh, sod off!"

"What? You are."

"Right, just because I bested the Crown Princess in a tournament, which makes us best mates."

"I wasn't talking about the princess."

"As important as I'm sure *this* is ..." Avery moved her hand in a circular motion, before she continued, "I think we should focus on Leyton and the pendant."

"Did you have any luck determining why someone might want it, aside from sentimental or monetary value?" Emerys sipped from her mug, grasping it with her whole hands.

"I found some old boxes of stuff my parents sent after I moved here. I think they were clearing out their place before they downsized. Anyway, I hadn't looked at it. I figured it was just junk from elementary school or things like that. But it turns out it contained a family history of the pendant."

"And your magic goes back generations I'm assuming?"

"I honestly don't know. My mom is a witch. Though my grandparents on both sides died before I was born. But the pendant is older than that ... a lot older." She finally realized she was holding an empty mug and filled it from the carry-out box. "There were some bills of sale in there and some appraisals, too. I knew it had some decent stones in it, but the most recent appraisal from about ten years ago valued it at ten thousand dollars."

I let out a whistle. "For a guy who just got fired from his dead-end job, ten grand would be a pretty sweet pay day."

"But how would he know its value before taking it?" Avery rubbed at her throat, as if the phantom memory of him ripping it free from the chain was still fresh.

"Did you talk about it with anyone recently? Bring it up at all?"

"No. I hadn't even thought about it in years."

"But you were wearing it yesterday. Out in public just for a stroll."

"I don't know. It just seemed like I really needed to have it with me.."

"Was anything out of the ordinary leading up to yesterday? You stated you felt this was coming. That your husband warned you?" Emerys stepped closer to Avery.

"In dreams. Des told me not to worry, because there was something bigger coming for me. That I was meant to do something really important." She gestured with the rim of her coffee mug at us. "I assumed it was meeting you all."

"Did he appear to you and tell you to wear the pendant?"

"Not that I remember and believe me, I don't forget dreams featuring my husband." After a beat she added, "Now that I think about it though, I think I was having dreams about the pendant lately. Like somehow my subconscious reminded me it existed."

"Serena said that Leyton might have gotten into

some gaming group. Could you have crossed paths that way? Maybe you were talking loot in a game or something?" Jules suggested.

"I have been doing a bit more gaming lately." She frowned, drumming her fingers on the outside of the mug. "You think someone could have gotten to me through a game?"

"I mean, you basically marry magic and tech for a living. It stands to reason someone else could do that, too," I pointed out. "And it's not beyond the realm of possibility, seeing as we literally had a magical cyberattack in Camelot."

"It feels too much like a coincidence, your network going down there and the possibility of me getting magically hacked here."

"Perhaps it is not a coincidence. Since Nim's attack, the barrier hasn't kept others from crossing into this realm."

I didn't need reminders of the Seelies who'd tried to steal the chalice from us. Or the soldiers who'd taken Nim from me. Still, if the Seelies were after the pendant, why leave witnesses? They hadn't been shy about leaving a trail of bloodshed behind them.

"Maybe they've been here longer than we realized," I said softly.

"What do you mean?" Emerys eyed me warily.

"We know that others have come through a long time ago, even hundreds of years. Seelies are just as good at living a really long time as dragons. So, why couldn't they hide out? Maybe they weren't sent by Uther originally, but for all we know, news of my return reached them and they're trying to help their king."

"That would make more sense if the pendant could do something that helped the Seelies," Jules noted.

"Yeah, you're going to want to see the boxes I found. I think it might explain exactly why someone would want it. And why they'd be willing to use hired guns to do their dirty work."

TWELVE

Fortified with coffee and baked goods, we crowded around the small two-person table in the kitchen. Avery produced a pair of handwritten journals that a quick skim told me went back at least one hundred and fifty years. She set a few more documents on the small surface and turned to her phone, running her finger over the screen as she read through some notes.

"So, from what I could figure out, the pendant was first gifted to my great-great-great-great grandmother in 1867. It might have been a wedding present as there is some reference to it being received right before she and her husband married."

"Being a gift could mean many things," Emerys said, bending over to scrutinize one of the appraisal documents. "This does say it was made of twenty-four karat gold and had a large amethyst pendant. Estimated value of ten thousand dollars."

"What does it say about the gift? Anything about who it was from?" I picked up one of the journals. Studying the delicate script on the page from an entry dated 17 May 1867, I read it aloud.

17 May 1867

I cannot believe our good fortune.
Father insists we cannot keep the pendant as it would arouse too many suspicions. We are not people of great means and yet it has been presented as a gift for my impending nuptials.

It is unlike anything I have seen before. I dare not touch it without a gloved hand for fear of tarnishing the jewel or the gold. I do wonder about its provenance as no one we know could afford such an exquisite object.

Mother believes me blessed beyond measure and insists that I must wear it on my wedding day. She says it will bring me great fortune and blessings for my marriage.

However, I cannot deny that being near it gives me an odd sense of peace.

"It doesn't say much about who gave her the pendant. But it does sound like something strange was going on with it."

"There was an entry before that … I flagged it," Avery said and gestured for me to flip the pages back.

I did so until I found the tiniest sliver of sticky note protruding from a page. The brief entry was dated 22 February 1867.

22 February 1867

I fear we will be made to leave our home and end my engagement with Michael. I meant no harm, but Mother fears I have been seen performing magic by our neigh-bors. I attempted to assure her that it was merely a simple washing spell, but she warned that women like us were burned and hung for such crimes.

I know that I need be fearful that Michael knows the truth. I have witnessed him perform such spells in our brief time unchaperoned. Mother may have given up on *her gift, but the magic lives on in me and will pass to our children. We have been blessed by the universe and 'tis our duty to give back.*

Well that answered the question of how far back Avery's ancestral magic went. At least three generations, likely more. And it also suggested why someone might have gifted her ancestors what appeared to be a magical pendant. They had either known about their abilities or suspected it. But it did beg the question as to what exactly the pendant *could do*.

"Were there any other entries that talked about the pendant and its abilities?" I scanned the rest of the journal, keeping an eye out for sticky notes that might give me a hint of where to look.

"Yeah, it looks like there was one towards the end, I wrote down the date. Check for June 16," Avery answered, glancing at her phone.

I flipped back to the end of the journal where the entries grew shorter still and further spaced out. Apparently, our author had less time to devote to documenting her innermost thoughts. I found the entry dated 16 June 1867.

16 June 1867

I have not yet processed the events following my wedding to Michael. I cannot put into words what I witnessed and yet I must try, so that I can hope to protect myself and my family.

Following our celebrations, we prepared to return to our new home when we were accosted by a group of angry citizens, claiming I had somehow cursed their water supply. Despite our refusal to the contrary, they insisted they would take action against us. One brute moved to strike me down and yet he could not lay a hand on me. So, long as I held fast to Michael, he too was unharmed.

At first, I could not discern what magic would have protected us. And then, as we fled for our lives, I felt the weight of that strange gift against my breast. It warmed to my touch and in an instant, I understood it had given us protection.

We must leave this place for our safety. I have begged Mother and Father to join us, as I fear they will be accosted, but they refuse to leave the place they have always *known. I do not wish to abandon my blood, but I must look to the future. We must do all we can to ensure the continuation of our lineage.*

"Sounds like they got cornered by an angry mob, but something protected them," Jules noted.

I looked up from the book and back to Avery. "You wouldn't happen to have a photograph of her on her wedding day?"

"Anything we did have would be in the same box where these came from. Let me get it."

That left Jules, Emerys, and I standing together in the kitchen. "It sounds like the pendant shielded her from harm," Emerys said.

It did indeed.

"But why would someone want to give this random family protection?"

"We still don't know who might have been the benefactor," Emerys continued. "There is also no clear evidence to support that whoever gifted the pendant knew of its abilities."

"Wait, I thought we weren't dealing in coincidences," Jules replied. "I believe whoever handed it over to them knew it had power."

Just because they knew it had power didn't

necessarily mean they knew the specifics of what it could do. What had happened to Avery's great-great-great grandparents might have been an accident. Or possibly a test.

"I wish we could have had a proper look at the pendant before it was snatched," I sighed.

"What do you think you could have gleaned from it?" Emerys pressed.

"I don't know. Maybe nothing. But maybe if it really was a magical artifact, I don't know ... Excalibur could have reacted with it somehow."

At that moment, Avery returned carrying the box she'd mentioned. A couple of faded black and white images were balanced on the lid. She set it atop the table and handed the photos over. "These were what I could find."

A handwritten date on the backs suggested this was our author and her husband. The fact they stood outside a small church, and she wore a white dress, suggesting it was in fact their wedding day. Sitting neatly against the collar of her gown was the same pendant I'd seen in my visions that had led me to Avery.

"Either whoever gave this gift knew it might protect her, or they hoped it would."

"That tracks with the other entries I found from

some of my more recent relatives. One was in San Franscisco during the 1906 earthquake, and they nearly died. Except the debris somehow missed them when their house collapsed. And another relative who'd been involved in a horrific car accident. Somehow, they came away nearly unscathed."

"Well, now we know that the pendant grants protection. That explains why someone would want it," I said, eyeing Avery. "Doesn't explain why they would just come take it off you. Or mind fuck you into handing it over."

"I actually read something in one of the later diaries about that," Avery set her phone down and grabbed the second diary. She flipped it open and handed it over.

21 November 1950

On this my twenty-first birthday, my mother presented me with a truly generous gift: the family pendant. I had often admired it whenever she or my grandmother wore it on holidays. But always at home. Never in public. I suspected it was because they feared someone might see its value and try to take it.

Oh, how I wish I'd followed that tradition now. I had just been to see Maureen and Lucille to celebrate, and I'd worn the pendant. They understandably gawked at it in wonder as it caught the light. It caught the eye of some low life on the street as we made our way back to my house. If I had been alone, I am almost certain he would have killed me. It was as if he were possessed. He reached for the pendant as if drawn to it and I could almost feel a power about the thing, something not of my own doing. As he grabbed for it his hands turned blistered and red. He howled in pain as if I'd tossed scalding water on him and he ran.

"It's got a defense mechanism, then," I murmured and set the book down. "So, why didn't that happen with Leyton?"

Avery shrugged. "Maybe it worked, and we just didn't know about it because we haven't been able to find him yet."

"And if it does, maybe it only attacks the first person who tries to take it from its rightful owner," Jules filled in, beginning to pace the short distance between the counter and the opposite wall. "So, whoever wanted it could have known about the protection and figured this bloke was someone no one would miss if he ended up wounded or dead."

"Not that I want to do him any favors, but his life is worth more than that," Avery countered.

"All of this is speculation until we locate the man and ask him ourselves." Emerys' tone came across matter of fact and determined.

"We should go by his flat and see if he's laying low." I pointed to Avery's phone. "Serena said the address in that police file was current."

"And what do you suggest we do if he is there?" Avery didn't sound convinced we should be chasing the man down at his home.

"We make him tell us everything he knows," Jules interjected.

"Or at the very least we see if he's got the pendant with him. Maybe we can just resolve things peacefully." I doubted the reality of my own words, but I still felt compelled to voice it. Maybe the universe would be kind for once and make things simple.

"Then we should get going." Emerys had already donned her coat and was halfway to the front door.

By some small miracle, Leyton's flat wasn't far from where Avery lived. It lent credence to the idea that he could have been spying on her or was targeted as someone conveniently located to her. As we approached the building, I fell into step beside Emerys.

"If the Seelies are behind this and they can

somehow make this protection spell work for them, we're fucked, aren't we?"

"I wouldn't go quite that far, but it would certainly complicate a great many things," Emerys answered.

"Bloody hell, I'm getting really tired of those fuckers. We've not done a thing to them, so why do they think they can just come along and take what isn't theirs?"

"Because Uther has always believed he deserves more than was given to him. He is power hungry and his need to conquer is unmatched in Albion."

Without intending to do so, my hands balled into fists as I pictured the Seelie King's face in my mind's eye. I'd love to give him a slug or two to the jaw.

"It's a walk-up," Avery said, interrupting my brooding.

I glanced at the row of tiny buttons labeled with flat numbers and then took a step back to glance upward. I spotted open curtains on the second floor and pressed the button for 2B. The intercom rang twice before a woman answered.

"Yeah?"

"Package delivery," I said in a horrible attempt at an American accent.

"I don't have any packages coming."

"Oh, so sorry about that ma'am. Looks like it's for your neighbor in 2C."

There was some grumbling on the other end of the connection before the woman said, "Tory is always forgetting when she orders things. Yeah, okay, come on up."

The door buzzed and Jules pulled it open, giving me an impressed smile. Avery and Emerys looked equally surprised, and I gave a sheepish grin. "It works in films."

It gave us the excuse we needed to get into the building and to Leyton's fourth floor unit. As we made the trek up several flights of stairs, I couldn't decide whether I wanted him to be there or not. I wanted this bloody quest done, so we could go home and rescue my kingdom from potential ruin. Yet I couldn't deny the thrill of being on the hunt for something magical. It fulfilled some little bit of adrenaline seeking I'd never let myself indulge before.

"Here we are." Avery's words came out in a whisper as we approached the door to 4A.

I tried the handle—locked. Unsurprising. I pressed an ear to the door and listened, holding my breath to catch any hints of movement. I thought I picked up the brief hint of a groan.

"He might be in there."

Jules shooed me back and pressed her hand to the doorframe. The handle turned almost molten as she worked literal magic to permit us entry into the flat. It wasn't something I'd seen her do before, but fully believed she was capable of doing. Then again, there was the time she'd spent in America where we'd been apart. She could have gotten up to all kinds of naughty things that never made it into her letters.

"Good thing we've got a federal agent on our side, seeing as we're breaking and entering right now," I said.

Avery gave a bitter laugh. "Yeah, Jacquie isn't exactly the type to look the other way most of the time. We'd better put things back the way we found them."

Noted.

Jules pushed the door inward and the scene that greeted us turned my stomach. The stench of anti-septic and illness filled my nose, choking off any clean air I might have been able to take in. I spotted smears of what looked like blood on one of the walls at arm height, sliding towards the ground. I moved ahead of the rest of our group. Layton lay curled in a tight ball on the floor not far from an open doorway leading to a toilet. He gave another groan and pressed his hand to his chest, cradling the blistering flesh.

"Well, I'd say we know for sure that taking the pendant by force ends up having some pretty nasty consequences."

Now we just had to hope we could get Leyton into some sort of state to help point us in the right direction. Time was running out.

CHAPTER

THIRTEEN

We needed to divide and conquer. As Leyton rocked on the floor, groaning in pain, I glanced around the small flat. It was sparsely furnished, and I could see things were amiss. Pillows and cushions from the couch lay scattered on the floor. And I spotted shards of broken glass leading into the small kitchenette. Beside me, Avery eased the door closed with her foot, careful not to touch the frame or handle.

"Could your friend help?" Emerys' words disrupted the unease that had settled over the place.

"Honestly, I don't know. He's done a lot of amazing things and he's a great Healer. But this, uh, I don't think anyone would have any idea how to treat this," Avery answered.

"Give him a ring and see anyway. We need Leyton to tell us what he knows," I said and stepped into the kitchenette.

The trail of broken glass came from a dish that sat discarded in the sink filled with dirty, soapy water. Like he'd tried to clean his hand injury. I didn't see evidence that anyone else had been here. That meant either he still had the pendant somewhere on the premises or he'd handed it off before coming home.

The fact the place appeared trashed suggested he'd come here with it first. Had whoever roped him into the theft already collected the pendant? I returned to the living room and knelt beside the man.

"Leyton, my name's Morgan," I said softly.

He groaned and grimaced in response, but he forced his eyes open. They were bloodshot and red-rimmed, but with some effort they focused on me. His brows knit together as confusion washed over him. "You were ..." His voice was hoarse.

"Yeah, we met," I filled in, hoping that by taking the lead in the conversation he'd save his strength. He weakly gestured to my stomach. "And I got better. Seems you're in a pretty bad way though."

"Didn't know ..." He strained to sit up, but his body refused to cooperate. "Just a .... job."

"You couldn't have known what the pendant would do when you tried to take it," Avery said, her tone lacking any hint of animosity. "I would bet whoever hired you to take it, they didn't fill you in on all the nitty gritty painful details."

He shook his head. "Hurts so bad."

"J.T.'s on shift. His phone went right to voice-mail," Avery said when I made eye contact with her.

"You've got to have other healers," Jules said.

"None I'd trust with this."

It meant we were going to have to get our hands dirty. I wasn't anything like a healer. Yet I had to believe that if I really needed it, my magic would do what was required; especially since I'd finally recon-nected with the source of it back in Camelot. I grabbed one of the discarded pillows and slid it under Leyton's head, trying to get him more comfortable.

"I'm going to try to help, but can't stop every-thing. I can't cure what's being done to you either, but I think I might be able to take the pain away for even just a little bit."

He nodded his consent, tears streaking his

cheeks. Emerys was at my side as I knelt on the hardwood next to him. "I am sorry to say I do not think there is anything we can do to save this man's life."

"I know." The words caught in my throat. "But that doesn't mean he's got to die alone and in agony."

"Don't want ... to die," Leyton croaked.

"Hush now. Just try to rest." It was the exact opposite of what I wanted. I really needed him to give me anything and everything he could about who he'd given the pendant to and where they were headed next.

I took his uninjured hand and held it within my own. Without meaning to, I pressed my left wrist to his hand so that the silver band that represented Excalibur's blade made contact with both of us. Almost instantly, without doing anything else, Leyton's breathing evened out and became less labored. Emerys disappeared briefly into the kitchenette, returning with a damp cloth. She sat on his other side and pressed the cloth to his face. I turned my attention to Avery and Jules.

"I'll try to keep him calm and comfortable. But one of you will need to see what you can get out of him."

Avery stood and gestured over her shoulder toward the bedroom. "I'll see if he's got a laptop or phone. Something we can use to trace who he's been in communication with."

She darted from the room before I could argue. That left Jules to be our interrogator. "Go easy on him."

"He nearly killed you, Morgan. You can't really expect me to go easy on him."

"I'm fine, Jules. All better, I promise. Now, just talk to him."

I gave Leyton's hand a firm squeeze to reassure him that he wasn't alone and to force myself to turn all of my attention to him. The taste of lime bubbled along my tongue as I reached across the space separating us and pulled away the waves of pain coming off him with each breath. He let out an almost contented sigh and his eyes fluttered closed.

"Leyton, I need to know if the pendant you took from Avery is still here," Jules said, crouching down in front of him.

"Not here," he replied.

"Where is it?"

"Don't know. They ... took it."

"Who took it? Who hired you for this insane job?"

"Didn't get ... names."

"You're lying!"

His hand trembled in mine, and I gave it another squeeze. "Maybe there's another way we can do this," I said and moved to sit across from Leyton while still holding tight to his hand. "Did you see who trashed your place?"

He nodded.

"Good. That's good. We're just going to try and take a little walk through that memory. Nice and simple."

His whole body shuddered in response to my words, but I was committed now. The question-and-answer session wasn't going to get us what we needed, and I could feel his pulse beginning to slow. Taking a deep breath in through my nose and out through my mouth, I shifted my magic's focus from easing his pain to getting inside his head.

His grip stiffened against my fingers as my magic tried to pry into his mind, to see what he'd experienced. His body jerked away, and I nearly lost my grip on him. If it weren't for Emerys wrapping her arms around his shoulders to keep him still, I'd have lost the connection entirely.

"Leyton, I know it's not something you want to

relive, but it's going to help," Emerys said calmly. "It will ease your suffering."

The hint of lime intensified, zipping down my arms like an electrical current as it bridged the gap between me and him. Something that I could almost identify as rotting basil rose up in response, putting up a barrier. His magic, tainted as it was by a defensive spell running through him, was trying to protect him.

We don't have time for this.

I pushed and my magic surged forward, poking holes in his defenses. It wasn't enough to fully get into his mind, but I could see snippets of images flashing through at two times speed.

A tall, dark-haired man with some sort of neck tattoo stood over Leyton in the living room. He sneered and the image changed to Leyton laying face-down on the floor. Something akin to a claw showed in the corner of his vision, all shadowy and portending pain. It flashed to a glimpse of the pendant catching the sunlight outside as the figure vanished.

Leyton's body stiffened as the images faded and his skin grew damp and clammy against mine. Emerys held tight to his torso, and I reached up, pressing my fingers to the side of his neck.

"He's got a really weak pulse."

"Should we phone an ambulance?" Jules sounded unnerved.

"I doubt they'd get here in time, and we don't need to get mixed up with the law, remember?" I answered.

"You aren't going to just let him die," she countered.

"I can't save him. What makes you think mundane medicine can counteract whatever is going on here?"

The floorboards creaked under Avery's weight as she reappeared in the doorway between the main living room and the bedroom. She held a thin laptop to her chest. I noticed an additional rectangular bulge in her pocket.

"I may have friends in law enforcement, but I don't think we want to be caught here," she said.

"What if we contact authorities anonymously? Report an injured man at this address?" Emerys suggested. "They may arrive too late, but he would not be alone."

Leyton clawed at me with his injured hand, breath rattling in his chest. He was surprisingly strong for a man at death's door, and I had to fight to pry his oozing fingers from my wrist. There were no good options here as we watched Leyton struggle to breathe.

"We stay until it's over," I said quietly. "That way he won't be alone."

We could report it after the fact. We'd tried to be careful not to touch things that might leave finger-prints. We just had to hope they wouldn't check his body for evidence. It would have to be enough. I pointed to the front door. "You all can go if you want."

Avery wavered on the spot, casting a look down at Leyton before moving toward the door. She ducked her head as she waved a hand and the door opened. She stepped outside. I swallowed the bile rising in my throat at the thought of watching a man die and stayed put. Jules pivoted on the spot.

"I'll go make sure she's all right."

"Thanks."

Then it was just me, Emerys, and a dying man in the flat. She was quiet as she ran the damp cloth over his face again, making soft shushing sounds. Given how long she'd lived, I had no doubt she'd been bedside at more than one death. I forced myself not to close my eyes. I feared that if I did, I'd relive Nim's death, and I was in no place to fall into that pool of grief right now. Not when my kingdom was counting on me.

"You have done him a kindness," Emerys said and stood, taking the cloth with her.

I looked at her and then down at the man beside me. His chest no longer rose or fell. I leaned in close, but couldn't hear any sound of breathing. His pulse was gone.

"He didn't deserve this." Anger bubbled behind my breastbone, burning like acid.

"And we will make certain his death was not in vain. But we should go now. We have lingered here too long already."

Leyton's body slumped back against the pillow as I let go and led the way out into the hall. Avery was down on the landing below us. Jules stood a couple of steps above her.

"He's gone," I announced.

"Paramedics are on the way," Jules answered.

"That's our cue to leave then."

I made it down to the third-floor landing and stood next to Avery. "You, okay?"

"This is what it was like for Ezri and Des, seeing death happen first-hand, dealing with the aftermath of the violence."

"Not what any of us signed up for, I know. But

we need to leave. We can go back to your place, or somewhere else, but we can't be here when they show up."

"Authority Headquarters would be better for decrypting his technology."

"Then that's our next stop."

"Did you manage to get anything from him before he died?" Jules bumped my shoulder as we descended to the first floor.

"Fragments. Not sure they'll do us any good though."

I wasn't willing to admit it, but the fresh morning air was a relief after the scent of death in Leyton's flat. The air was cool and crisp, smelling of gasoline and cheap coffee. It wasn't home, but it was urban enough to soothe my nerves a bit. Getting back to the Authority's base of operations meant a trip on public transit or a cab ride. Neither thrilled me. Ultimately, we crammed into Avery's VW Bug for the trek.

"Sorry you're so squished back there," Avery said as she caught my reflection in the rearview mirror.

"It's fine," I answered as Jules' elbow lodged in my ribcage.

"This was Des' baby, and I haven't had the heart to sell it."

I was about to reiterate that it was fine when the circular drive appeared before us. She pulled in and around to park at the front of the entryway. Jules and I spilled out of the vehicle's small confines, and I straightened with a groan as my spine realigned itself.

"What do you think's going on back in Camelot?" Jules asked as Avery led the way up the steps and inside.

"Honestly, I've been trying not to think about it."

"Afraid you'll spiral into worst case scenarios?"

"That's about the heart of it. We're cut off from them in a way and that's almost worse than just their networks being down. And until recently I never even considered it was a thing that could happen. "

"We'll get back and figure out how to save them. You're the Chosen One after all. It's pretty much in your job description, right?"

"Guess it is."

The space was quieter than the last time we'd been there and that was difficult, since I was fairly certain I hadn't seen anyone not affiliated in some way with our group when we'd last been here. Avery stopped at the door that led to the Council Chamber meeting room and knocked. I picked up on the sound of chairs scraping against the floor and the door opened.

"Sorry, we're in session," a young woman stated.

"I just need to get to the tech room," Avery replied. "Trust me, it's important."

The woman glanced at the rest of us with a wary expression before opening the door wide enough to let us in. Most of the seats in the semi-circle were filled this time and I felt a dozen pairs of eyes tracking my movements as I walked through. It was only then that I realized my clothes likely smelled and I had some suspicious stains on my sleeves. I'd left my pack of fresh clothes at Avery's place. However, cleaning up was the least of our worries right now as I marched on through, trying to hold my head high as if there was nothing wrong with how I looked.

Despite the cramped quarters, the four of us squeezed into the tech room. Avery plugged in Leyton's laptop and phone into waiting cords. The monitor flickered, displaying a larger version of the screen asking for a password.

"I don't suppose your magic means you're an expert hacker, does it?" I asked hopefully.

Avery gave me a smile that was equal parts sadness and mischief. "Before I moved out here, I may have dabbled in some grey hat stuff. Snooping through surveillance footage is going to look like child's play."

We just had to hope that Avery's skills were up to the task. Otherwise, our leads had just died with the man in the flat.

CHAPTER

FOURTEEN

I wasn't sure what to expect when Avery turned her attention to the computer's lock screen. I doubted she'd found his password taped to the underside of a desk drawer. And it wasn't like I'd gotten anything from Leyton that would give us a hint as to how to access his tech.

"I don't want to put more pressure on you, but we do have a deadline," Jules said when Avery had sat immobile for a good five minutes.

Avery opened her eyes and looked over her shoulder. "I'm fully aware there's a deadline, thank you."

"Then why are you just sitting there?"

"Why don't we give Avery some space?" I suggested and nudged Jules towards the door.

Emerys followed my lead and opened it. "I think Morgan is correct."

Jules let out an irritated huff, but left the room with Emerys hot on her heels. That left Avery and I in the space alone. I started for the door, too, but she reached out her hand to grab mine.

"You can stay."

"I would just be in the way," I protested.

"When I'm breaking magical codes, I always do it with a partner. You never know what might be hiding just out of sight. I need someone to have my back."

"And you said you prefer to work with people whose magic you know."

"And I know yours now."

"You really think Leyton was sophisticated enough to have that sort of magic protecting his laptop?"

"Honestly, I don't know and it's the part that worries me. From the outside, it looks like he's just a guy that got in over his head and paid a price he'd never expected to pay. But people are complicated and layered."

"I'll stay, just tell me how I can help."

"Pull up a chair and just sit for now."

I did as she instructed and settled shoulder-to-shoulder with her at the desk. I could feel her magic building as she worked. She pressed her hand to the screen just like she'd done the other day when accessing the video footage. But this time, the screen remained black. Her brow furrowed and she let out a soft, "Huh."

I hesitated to interrupt her, but the sound of her curiosity was too much for me to ignore. "Find something already?"

"Just that you were right, and it wasn't as complicated as I thought. His password was pineapple."

"Seriously?"

She pulled her hand away from the screen and the pixels resolved into the lock screen asking for a password. She typed the word 'pineapple' in and hit the enter key. The computer gave a pleasant chime as it unlocked and revealed Leyton's digital life laid out for us. His computer didn't have a ton of programs, although I did note it had a lot of processing power for a simple machine.

"He probably modified this to work more like a gaming computer," Avery said mostly to herself. "Let's see where he's been online lately."

With a few keystrokes, she opened up a browser and pulled up a history of everywhere he'd been in the last couple of weeks. There was a forum of some sort for an online game I'd never heard of that came up more than a dozen times.

"I'm going to go out on a limb and say that's where they found him."

She navigated to the page and easily found his private messages—thanks to the password save, we didn't have to crack this one—and found two message threads with recent dates. She picked the older thread and started skimming. A lot of it was written in code, or at least it looked that way to me. But I wasn't a gamer.

"Anything useful in there?" I prompted.

"Oh, they definitely groomed him for this. They promised him a bunch of in-game bonuses if he helped them out in the real world."

"Any evidence they made good on those promises?"

"Looking at his reserves in-game, no. There are no large transfers. My guess is that once they got what they wanted and found him in the state he was in, there wasn't a need to keep up the pretense."

"What about that other thread?"

"Looks like he made a friend. Something more normal. Lots of talk about the game itself and strategy. Looked like they were planning to team up for some mission soon."

"So, nothing helpful."

"Oh, I don't know about that." She scrolled up to the most recent messages from the other person whose handle read ViperWraith. It showed a series of unanswered messages from them to Leyton asking why he hadn't been on in a few days.

"Do you think Leyton told them about what he was planning to do?" My words came out in a rush.

"I mean it looks like there's a chat function that you can use while you're actually playing, but it doesn't store afterward."

"So, we have no idea?"

"Well, there is one way to find out."

I didn't like the glint in her eyes. "Please don't tell me you want to pretend to be Leyton."

"Nope. You are."

"Bullshit. You know I am not a gamer. I'm a bloody bartender. Ask me about cocktails or wine vintages and I'm your girl. Online gaming, I wouldn't know where to start. They'd spot me as a fraud a mile off."

"Not if I'm giving you the answers."

"Why does it have to be me?"

"Because there's a chance that Leyton clued

Viper in on who I am. If they shared photos in chat or anything, they'd know something was up."

"There is also the small problem that I'm not a bloke."

"From these messages it's unclear whether Viper knew that Leyton was a guy. Besides, plenty of women play male characters. Sometimes, it's the only way they get taken seriously."

I didn't have trouble believing that point. It also probably helped that the male characters in most games had decent clothing and armor rather than the barely there female characters' clothing. Still, I doubted my ability to grift believably.

"I think we should just let you do this and take the risk that he showed your picture to this Viper person," I protested.

"I believe you can do this. Besides, we want them to cooperate with us, not feel antagonized if the person their buddy was supposed to steal from shows up demanding information."

"What if they don't even want to meet in person?"

"Then it's even easier since you can definitely bluff your way through a text conversation," she replied cheerily.

I swallowed my nerves and gave her a nod. "All right. Let's see if Viper wants to meet up."

Avery set her fingers to the keys and typed out a message apologizing for not responding sooner, because they'd been busy dealing with the fallout.

> The story is epic. Better if I told you
> in person.

The little circle around Viper's avatar turned from a pale blue to a bright green, signaling they were online and reading the messages. Tiny dots showed up at the bottom of the screen signaling they were typing.

> You sure you're ready for that?

> Think I finally am.

There was another pause as Viper typed.

> Name the place.

Avery looked at me. "We want a place we can control."

"Somewhere like the park would work. Lots of open space, more privacy."

"But that gives them too many ways to get out if they want to avoid us."

"Where do you suggest?"

"Notre Dame."

"Oh, fuck no. That prick of a bartender would sooner have me arrested if I set foot back in his bar."

"Relax, I'll get Molly to sweet talk him into agreeing."

I didn't have the time to ask who Molly was or why she held such sway over the man I'd clashed with.

"If you think it will work."

She flashed me a smirk before typing her reply to Viper.

> There's a bar I used to work at called Notre Dame. Meet there tonight, eight o'clock. I'll be at the last table in the back.

Viper's reply came slower this time, like they had to really contemplate what they wanted to do. My palms grew sweaty as the screen remained devoid of a confirmation, or more questions.

> I'll be there.

"Now we just have to hope that whoever this ViperWraith is, they can lead us to the bastards who hired Leyton."

Avery pivoted in her seat and appraised me. "Yeah, you're going to need a wardrobe change first."

"What's wrong with my clothes?"

"I mean, generally, nothing. But they're very 'I'm going to kick your ass' and that's great. But you walk into the bar looking like this and they really will know you aren't a gamer."

"Is this the part where you tell me that you can make me over?"

"Well, I have always wanted to do an epic makeover montage," she joked.

I checked the time. It was only noon now. We had plenty of time to get me made over and secure our location. "Fine. Remake me in your gamer image."

———

WE MADE it back to Avery's flat by two o'clock with lunch and a little light shopping. I sat in the bedroom as she sorted through shirts. Emerys and Jules were in the other room conspiring in low voices. I got the sense neither of them was pleased about me putting myself out there like bait.

"You know, you really aren't what I'd expect for a

princess," Avery commented as she held up a shirt to see if it was the right one.

"Didn't grow up as one," I replied. "My Aunt Nim raised me here back in London."

"So, she was royalty, too?"

"No. Actually, she wasn't a blood relative at all. She was meant to kill me as a baby, but she couldn't do it. She ran and brought me here where she thought I'd be safe."

"Wow. That's ... a lot."

"Gets better. About four months ago, I finally made it home again and had to dethrone the asshole who'd been living in my place all this time. A real piece of work called Arthur."

"Lots of drama. Is it always going to be that intense?"

I gave her a sobering look. "Part of me wants to say no, but given how the last few months have gone, I can't see it calming down for very long. Not when the Seelies are trying to end our existence or steal our crown at every turn."

"Is that just a different kingdom or ..." she trailed off. "The way you say it, I don't know, it sounds like a different species."

"I never thought about it that hard before, but I guess they are different from us. They don't age, or at least they take a really long time to grow old. They've got pointed ears and most of them can't be trusted."

"Most?"

"Like I said, Nim saved my life and raised me like I was her own. But she never let me forget where I really came from."

"You mentioned dragons, too."

"They're the good ones. At least the ones I've met so far. They've been honorable, noble, and kind. And beautiful. I mean some are the most strikingly handsome people I've ever met."

"I wonder if I'll get to meet one someday."

"I'd say you've got a pretty high chance. Honestly, I wouldn't be surprised if Taron swoops in the minute we're back through the barrier."

"Taron?"

"Former Crown Prince of the Dragons. He gave up the throne for his sister. He'd rather hang around his cave and build things."

"I take it he's one of the strikingly handsome ones?"

Heat warmed every part of my body. "Yeah, you could say that."

"Well, I look forward to meeting him when this is all over and we've saved your kingdom." She held up a different shirt and gave it an approving nod. "Here, change into this."

She left me alone to change out of my shirt and pants. At least she'd let me keep the boots. I tugged the graphic t-shirt over my head and settled it against my torso. The neckline was higher than I was used to, but not uncomfortable. I pulled on the bracelets she'd left for me, making sure to put them on my right wrist. The sapphire at the heart of Excalibur circling my left wrist warmed against my skin.

"I know you've felt left out. Something tells me before this is over, you'll get your chance to shine."

A soft knock came at the door, and I looked up to find Jules standing there. I motioned for her to come in and she sat beside me, wrapping her arms around my shoulders.

"I'm sorry," she said into my shoulder.

"For what?"

"For being a bitch lately. I don't know, I think maybe I'm just a little jealous."

"You're being daft."

"I see you with her and I don't see a place for me."

"Oh, come off it, Jules. You're my best mate. No one is going to change that. Not in a million years.

But I think it's pretty obvious we're going to need some extra help to stop Arthur and his batshit crazy father from ruining our lives."

"I know. I just haven't had to share you before. Not like this anyway."

"We'll get through it," I assured her and leaned over to plant a light kiss on the top of her head. "Besides, I wouldn't even be here without you."

"Yeah, that is basically true." After a beat she added. "Emerys and I talked it over and we're going to be at the bar as your backup."

"Wouldn't have it any other way. Just have to hope the bloody brute of a bartender doesn't get his knickers in a twist about us doing this in his bar."

"You just don't like that he's as good as you at tending bar."

"What? I am not mad about that. I haven't had a drink in his bar to compare. He's just a dick."

Avery appeared in the doorway. "We're set for tonight." She held up a tiny box and tossed it at me overhand.

I caught it, flipping open the lid. A tiny flesh-colored earpiece sat nestled inside against some pristine white padding. "I feel like a proper spy now. Where's my Aston Martin, Q?"

"Well then I guess it's time to go play Princess,

Witch, Hacker, and Spy," Avery said with a laugh and a broad grin.

For someone who'd been unable to be in the presence of a dying man only a few hours ago, she was awfully chipper about the whole bloody thing. Maybe it was her way of coping with the trauma. I no doubt would be seeing Leyton in my dreams for a while. I just had to find the bastards who'd used him and make them pay for ruining the man's life. There was no way in hell I was going to let the Seelies get their hands on such potent magic.

I twisted my hair up into a knot at the nape of my neck and donned a pair of glasses with non-prescription lenses in them. I turned to Jules, and she gave me an approving nod.

Time to go ensnare a viper.

FIFTEEN

The atmosphere of Notre Dame was less headache-inducing this time around. Maybe the music really was less intense, or I was just better prepared for the ambiance. Or maybe I was no longer seen as a threat by the proprietor? No matter, I was grateful that my skull wasn't trying to split down the middle when I arrived at quarter to eight. I'd fretted that we should have arrived earlier, but Avery assured me that we would be fine. I walked up to the bar, drumming my fingers along the wooden surface, catching Emerys and Jules moving farther into the interior to find a high-top table to lounge at nearby. It wasn't close enough to overhear my conversation once I moved to the last table, but at least they had a solid view of the entrance and the back.

"You really shouldn't be drinking at a time like this," Avery's voice came through the earpiece nestled in my left ear.

"I wasn't going to actually drink it." *Much.*

"Talking to yourself isn't a good look," Jonathan said, appearing as if out of thin air.

I gestured to my ear. "Not talking to myself. And I'll take a pint of your darkest."

"Coming right up." He filled the beer glass with more flourish and finesse than I'd expect before setting it on the bar between us. "And just because I agreed to let you do whatever this is in my bar, doesn't mean you get a free pass. That's fifteen bucks."

Now I knew how our patrons back home felt about our prices. I glared at him, but handed over the twenty dollar bill Avery had given me for emergencies. "I promise I won't blow up your precious bar."

"I'll hold you to that, Princess."

"Oh, fuck off!"

That earned me a genuine smile as he moved on to attend to other patrons. I took my beer and artfully maneuvered through the crowd toward the rear. As promised, he'd ensured the table at the very back was empty. I slid into the seat facing the entrance. My phone ticked over to eight o'clock and my gaze shifted to the front door, my body flinching every time someone new entered the space.

"Take a deep breath. You got this," Avery's voice chimed in my ear. It had to be fueled by magic for me to hear her so clearly above the background noise of the bar.

"How am I even supposed to know who we're looking for?"

Just then, a woman walked in, and she stood out for two reasons. First, she was dressed eerily similar to what I wore, and second, she had a visible forearm tattoo of a giant snake wrapped around a reaper's scythe. I took a sip from my beer and straightened a little.

"I think I've got our girl after all."

From across the bar, I spotted Jules flashing me a thumbs up as she bopped along to the music. Emerys leaned against the table, watching the crowd. Despite the fact she was over eight hundred years old, she looked remarkably hip and like she could slide onto the dance floor with the rest of them without a problem.

I turned my attention back to the woman with

the tattoo as she scanned the crowd and moved slowly towards the back of the establishment. She scanned each table as she got to the rear, no doubt looking for a man. I noted a laptop bag slung over one shoulder as she approached. I fiddled with the glasses as they slipped down my nose and made a move to stand slowly, offering a shy wave.

The woman's gaze narrowed in on my gesture and then widened in surprise. She stopped mid-stride for a beat before closing the distance between us at an even slower pace.

"Viper?" I called over the noise.

"KingMaker?"

For a split second I had no idea what she was talking about. Then I remembered that was Leyton's handle in the game. "Bit of a surprise I know."

"Yeah. I didn't know you were a girl."

"Not a girl. I'm a woman," I corrected.

"I just meant ... you aren't what I was expecting." She stood on the other side of the table and watched me. "I've been screwed before."

"I get it." I held up the phone in front of me and unlocked it, showing off the game's mobile version with the message thread between Leyton and Viper. It had been Avery's idea to change the Touch ID to my fingerprint just to sell the ruse.

Her shoulders sagged a little with relief and she sat down. "You scared me, going dark like that for so long."

"Things got a little out of hand and I needed to lay low."

"I still can't believe you agreed to help those guys. It sounded stupid. You could have been arrested."

Oh, if only you knew.

"Tell her that you regret what you did and that you would like her help to make it right," Avery's voice came through the earpiece.

"I've been thinking a lot about what I did, and I know it was wrong. I want to make it right. Wouldn't you want to do the same?"

"How do you think you're going to do that?"

"Maybe find the guys who hired me and demand what I took back?"

"King, I did some digging into the guys you were talking to and there's something weird about them." She leaned in closer. "I don't think they even play the game."

"How do you know? And even if they don't, so what?"

"I think they used you and the game to do their dirty work."

"Can you help me? You clearly did more research than I did. I was hurting and just took the first offer that came along."

"Say you could get this thing back that you took, how would you even know where to find the woman again?"

"I'd know."

"It seems kind of dangerous. Maybe you should just cut your losses and walk away from this one. These guys feel dangerous, the kind that could really get you hurt. No chance to use healing points in the real world to make it better."

My mouth went dry at her words. She understood the danger that Leyton had found himself in far better than he had. Had she tried to warn him off? Or was she trying to assuage her conscience now? That would be more believable if she was aware that she wasn't actually talking to the person she believed to be KingMaker.

"I can't do this," I muttered loud enough for Avery to pick up.

"You've barely got her trust as it is, Morgan. You tell her the truth now and we're done. We'll lose whatever information she's got," Avery argued.

Across the table, Viper stared at me, clearly registering something was going on. I inhaled deeply through my nose and blew the breath out through my mouth. "You're right, it was dangerous. Those guys were the kind you don't come back from."

She leaned back in her chair, her body language telegraphing that she was preparing to run. "What?"

I pulled off the glasses. "I'm sorry. But I'm not the person you've been talking to in the game."

"You have their phone."

"That's true. But that's because he won't be needing it anymore."

"What did you do?"

"I tried to help him. And given what he did to me, some people might think I was mental for even offering a helping hand."

"You aren't the person KingMaker was supposed to go after. They sent me a picture, too. She was blonde."

"Also, true. I happened to be in the right place at the wrong time. Ended up on the other end of your mate's knife, after he'd robbed her."

"So, what is this, some sort of extortion?"

"No. When I said I wanted to get back what was stolen, I meant it. The people who hired your friend … they let him die. They used him to get around some pretty nasty defenses and then they took it, not caring what happened to him. I'm trying to make his death mean something."

"And you expect me to believe this?"

"You should get over here," I addressed Avery.

In the next moment, the woman across the table from me was on her feet. Only when she turned to leave, Jules and Emerys flanked her.

"We don't want to hurt you. We think you cared for Leyton and would want to honor him," Emerys said gently, not raising a hand or her voice.

Over Emerys' right shoulder I spotted Avery weaving her way through the crowd. She looked uncomfortable that I'd forced her into this situation in the flesh. But I couldn't explain the value of the pendant as well as she could. Besides, Avery was the one who suffered the harm here.

"This is Avery. She's the one your friend robbed," I introduced.

"Yeah, you look like the picture."

"I am really sorry we tried to lead you on. It wasn't right and that's on me. I put Morgan up to it," Avery said.

"You just wanted your stuff back," Viper replied.

"I don't know how much you really knew about Leyton," Avery continued.

"That was his real name?"

"Yes. Leyton Danson. He actually used to work here. He, uh ... was targeted in the game. The people who hired him knew he had certain skills they could exploit."

"You mean because he had magic," she replied.

"You knew?"

"I mean, they ... he told me he did. I figured he was just making it up."

"Well, sorry to break it to you, but magic is very real and can be very deadly. It's what ended up killing him," I said. My admission earned me a horrified look from Avery. We didn't have time to beat around the bush. If a mundane had to learn the truth, so we could finish what we came for, so be it.

"What is this thing he took from you anyway?"

"A very powerful pendant with one hell of a protection spell. And in the wrong hands, it could do a lot of damage."

"Like the guys who recruited Leyton."

"Exactly. We want to stop them from hurting anyone else and take back what they took. But we don't really know where to look. They didn't leave much of a trail to follow," Avery interjected.

"Yeah, they were pretty clever," Viper agreed. "I almost didn't find them myself."

"But you did?" I couldn't hide the hopeful note in my voice.

"Well, I mean, I found the IP address. Mapping tells me it's somewhere downtown, but I can't get any closer than that. You'd need something like law enforcement-level software for that sort of stuff."

I looked at Avery. "Might be time to call in that FBI friend of yours again."

Viper paled at the mention of the FBI. "Don't worry, she's on our side. And we won't say a word about anything questionable you might have had to do to track them down."

"This was not at all how I expected my night to go. We were friends online for years. I really thought we'd built some trust, you know? It wasn't even just a single game. We crossed platforms, sometimes just because the other was there. It was rare to find someone I had that kind of a connection with." She took a breath. "I want to help."

"Are you sure?" Jules and I spoke in unison, voicing a joint skepticism at her answer.

"He was my friend. Like you said, I owe it to him to make this right if I can."

"So, what's our next step?" Jules eyed Avery.

"We need to trace that IP address."

"What else did you find out about these guys?" I

addressed Viper. "You said they didn't play the game, but they had to have access to it somehow."

"That's kind of the weird thing. It was almost like they had admin-level access. Like they could hop in and out at the creator level."

"Wouldn't be the first time game designers gave themselves back doors into things," Avery muttered. "But that also means they'll be looking for intrusions. We'll have to be careful."

"I did see them pop up in a couple of private chats. I couldn't access them though. They had some sketchy name like The Inferno or something dramatic like that."

Given what they'd managed so far, it certainly felt like we were marching into the heart of an inferno. But that was the plight of the Chosen One, wasn't it? Being thrust into danger simply because we were destined to do so by fate or whatever?

"I think we ought to head somewhere a bit more private if we're going to continue this discussion," I suggested. While I didn't doubt that Jonathan's establishment had safeguards in place beyond those that kept people from committing violence or being a drunken prick, I assumed that eavesdropping was still plausible.

"It would be easier back at Headquarters," Avery said.

I checked the time. It was already after nine. "I don't think we can afford to make that trip again right now. Your flat will have to do."

"I'll call Jacquie on the way and fill her in." She looked at Viper, no doubt weighing our options. We needed the information she had, but we knew little about her and just inviting her to Avery's flat seemed a foolish move. Finally, Avery let out a breath and addressed the woman. "Guess you're coming with us."

Needing the fortification, I grabbed the beer and downed it in a few big gulps. Jules gave me a knowing smile as we left the bar behind and stepped into the cold November night. My head began to swim as we made the trip back to Avery's flat and it had nothing to do with the alcohol.

All this talk of technology, subterfuge, and hiding behind screens unnerved me. Maybe I was too used to people coming at me where I could actually defend myself.

"If I had one wish, it would be to have no more bloody people lurking behind screens. If they want to come at us, just do it to our faces," I announced from the passenger seat as Avery pulled into a parking space.

"Really, of all the things you could wish for, that's it?" Jules teased. "Not winning the lotto, or having Nim back?"

She had a point with the second one. "Tonight, no. Let the bastards show their faces, so we know what it is we're actually fighting. Otherwise, they're just cowards. And if I know anything about Seelies, it's that they hate being seen as weak."

A car pulled up on the street half a foot from Viper and she jumped, scurrying towards us as the driver's door opened. Agent DeWitt emerged.

"This better be the last time you come to me looking to borrow resources I shouldn't even be lending out." She gave Avery a pointed look.

"Something tells me it will be. And thank you for having my back. It really means a lot."

"If it helps get criminals off the street, I'm all for it." She gave Viper a passing glance before gesturing inside. "You said it was urgent I get here. So, let's not waste any more time talking about it."

I admired the woman's determination, and her no-nonsense approach was starting to rub off on me, too. Despite not knowing a bloody thing about what we were about to do, I marched inside like I had all the confidence in the world. Time to bring the fight to them.

SIXTEEN

"Staring at me isn't going to make this go any faster," Avery said as I hovered over her shoulder, trying to watch what she was doing.

"I just don't want to miss anything," I said, starting to pace.

"Trust me, there's not much to see right now." Avery looked across the living room to Agent DeWitt, who stood by one of the large windows with her phone pressed to her ear.

"We're going to have a small window to get this done," she said, turning back to Avery and handing over the phone. "He'll walk you through what you need."

Avery pressed the phone between her shoulder and ear, and typed, her fingers flying across the keyboard at light speed. I wasn't even sure her hands touched the keys. The air in the flat was thick with tension as Viper—who'd volunteered her real first name as Fran—stood at the other end of the couch. She watched Avery's every move like a hawk. I couldn't tell if she was trying to memorize the keystrokes or if she still didn't quite believe we were about to gain access to the FBI's database to track down her friend's killers.

"I think I'm in," Avery announced, setting Agent DeWitt's phone down on the table beside her.

I peered over her shoulder and looked at the screen again. It looked unchanged from what it had a moment ago, but Avery wore a triumphant expression. She eyed Fran and made a grabbing gesture. "Let me see the IP address you found."

Fran sat beside Avery on the couch and opened up her own laptop. She logged into the game that we'd seen on Leyton's computer and shared a screenshot she'd taken a day ago. "I just hope they haven't disappeared."

"We're going to get them," Avery promised.

"Unless there's concrete evidence these guys actually facilitated anything, I'm not sure what law enforcement can do," Agent DeWitt said.

"We all witnessed Leyton steal her pendant. That's assault and theft, isn't it?" I quipped.

"You willing to stick around and testify to that in court?"

That thought made the bottom drop out of my stomach. "They still deserve whatever karma delivers to them."

"That I don't disagree with."

"You all done with me, Jacquie?" a male voice came from the phone on the table. I hadn't realized Avery had set it to speaker.

"For now. Just keep an eye on things from your end and let me know if we get any unwanted attention." Agent DeWitt reached over and picked up the phone, ending the call and stowing the device in her jacket pocket.

"This might take a little while to pinpoint the exact address," Avery said and pointed to Fran's computer. "Want to see about cracking their encryption to get into those private conversations? It might be enough to prove they facilitated everything and that they intended to hang Leyton out to dry."

Fran swallowed audibly. "I'm not a hacker. Not really. I mean I code, and I can do a little bit of that sort of thing, but I'm really not that good."

"Lucky for you, Avery's a tech whiz," I offered, hoping to bolster the woman's spirits.

"No pressure," Jules offered from where she stood in the far corner.

"Will this trace back to me?" Fran's question came out soft and fearful.

"You should have some protection from our servers right now on your laptop. It might be easier to use with that too," Agent DeWitt suggested.

"Give me a second to get in." Avery's fingers moved over the keys at a slower pace this time round.

Another window popped up on Avery's screen, displaying the log-in screen for the game. Fran reluctantly entered her credentials and showed Avery where she'd uncovered the private conversations. After a few minutes of failed attempts, Avery sat back, pulling her glasses from her face and pinching the bridge of her nose.

"I'm missing something, I just don't know what."

"We're operating under the assumption they knew that your pendant was magic, right?" I said, continuing to pace.

"Yeah. So?"

"Well, if they know about a magical object and

they had to know that Leyton had magic to try and take it from you. And we assume that these are Seelies behind this." I caught Fran mouth the word in confusion. "Then what if the game has some magical component to it?"

"You think that whoever made the game actually coded magic into it?" Avery sounded almost impressed.

"I mean I've heard crazier things. And you've used magic to manipulate technology before, too. You can't be the only one who knows how to do it. Now, what reason they'd have to do this, I couldn't begin to guess."

"Usually, the simplest reason is the truest. Greed, control," Agent DeWitt said.

Sounded like the Seelies to me.

"Let me try looking at this from a more magical perspective." Avery closed her eyes, and I could swear her whole body began to vibrate.

The room around us shifted, much like it had when we'd gone into the video footage during our initial deep dive to identify Leyton. Except this time no people were strolling by, oblivious to what had happened to either of us. It was just a dark void.

"Uh, Avery, what the hell is this?"

Her eyes opened and she stood, moving to stand

beside me, having walked through the table if I wasn't mistaken. The rest of our companions appeared to have vanished. That made unease prickle along the nape of my neck.

"This is what I found when I tried to reach out to that private chat with magic."

"Nothing."

"No, not nothing." She held up a hand and pressed the space in front of her. It pixelated before resolving back into a solid mass. "I think it's meant to make people *think* there's nothing here."

"Okay, well how do we get past it then?"

"Well, if I wanted to make sure only the right people could gain access, then I'd want to be sure that they knew magic was real and that it can be used in conjunction with technology. And I'd want there to be safeguards in case people like us came along."

That didn't inspire me with confidence. That they'd be ready for an assault wasn't a surprise. But the fact that we were the ones mounting it and potentially facing whatever obstacles they had laid in our path worried me. I hated walking into things blind. For a brief moment I was back in Camelot, stepping into the tent for the qualifying trial for the tournament four months ago. I'd been unprepared

—or so I'd assumed—for that experience. I couldn't shake those same doubts now.

"How can I help?" I did my best to focus on what I could control.

"Just have my back. I don't know what sort of booby traps they're going to throw at us or what sort of fail safes they have in place."

I shook my arms out, trying to dispel any tension in my muscles. I flexed my fingers and felt my power rippling over my skin, ready to do my bidding. At least I wasn't suffering from performance anxiety.

"I'm ready."

Avery felt around in the inky darkness, her fingers slipping in and out of existence as she moved along the space. Finally, she stopped moving, her hand hitting something resembling a solid object— an ornate door with a series of ominous-looking locks. I watched as Avery concentrated and a skeleton key materialized in her other hand. She held it up, examining the handiwork before trying it in the lock closest to the handle.

An ear-splitting keening sound erupted around us, and I fell to my knees, pressing my hands into my ears to block out the sound. *What the fuck is that?* Something—maybe instinct—told me something was coming. I forced myself to pull my hands away and balled them into fists, ready to take a swing at whatever came next. The horrible sound continued and then two violet eyes materialized from the darkness, charging right at us. Not having a better option in the moment, I swung anyway, connecting with something ethereal. My hand came away covered in a thin layer of red mist. I shook my hand to get the mist off, but it clung to me.

Everything went red and hazy for a moment before my senses returned. The sound had ceased, but my ears still rang with the echo. The thing I'd hit skidded to a halt just past Avery who was busy fiddling with the skeleton key, trying to make it match the lock she wanted to undo.

The thing looked like a strange cross between a dog and a lizard. It had tufts of reddish fur on the tips of its ears and an elongated snout. Rows of sharp teeth somehow glistened in the dark and it rose onto its hind legs to stand. A vicious tail whipped out from behind it, striking like a scorpion. I raised both hands, managing to catch the creature's tail between my palms. I wrapped my fingers tight and yanked. It gave a howl of pain, but freed itself from my grasp. With its mouth fully open it let out another of those ear-splitting wails.

"Keep it distracted," Avery yelled. I saw she'd just managed to dismantle the first lock.

Only four to go. Grand.

"Come on, come and get me," I taunted.

It scraped its hind legs against what I assumed represented the floor and bent forward, ready to charge. *Idiot, don't encourage the murderous monster!* My left wrist grew hot as the thing came for me. I didn't need to look down to understand what was happening. Excalibur wanted in on the action.

"Not a moment too soon," I whispered and pressed my right index finger on the sapphire.

The bracelet transformed, replaced by the gleaming sword in an instant. I took up a defensive posture like Taron had taught me and raised the blade. The creature lunged and I struck its scale-covered belly with the side of the blade. It wasn't enough to do any real damage. Still, it caught the beast off guard enough and sent it tumbling away from me. In my peripheral vision, I could swear a second creature emerged from the darkness.

"Not to rush you, but I think we've got more company."

"I'm working on it," Avery replied.

I took my gaze off the pair of beasts long enough to see that she'd managed to undo a second lock.

"I don't know how long I can keep two of these things at bay," I noted.

A growl from behind pulled my attention away from Avery and I spun, bringing Excalibur up to defend against the attack. The creature's claws raked across my chest, leaving a trail of mist behind again. It took my breath away. I really needed to remember not to let these things touch me.

In front of me, the creature that had just tried to rip my chest open shimmered and split in two. Part of me wanted to believe it was a trick of my oxygen-deprived brain. But I blinked a few times, and the thing didn't resolve back into a single creature.

"Damn it," Avery groaned and pulled out the remnants of the key, the rest sticking out of the third lock.

"Want a trade?" I said through a cough.

Avery just shook her head and waved her hands in front of her, producing something more akin to lock picks. "I was trying to be too nice. Time to brute force this."

Just facing these things head on as they decided to come at me wasn't going to be a winning strategy. I needed to go on the offensive. Having no idea what these things were even supposed to be, I couldn't fathom what might distract them. So, I'd have to contain them. It would be better if I could find a way to get them to turn on each other, but that didn't seem to be in the cards. I shifted Excalibur back to my left hand and raised my right, sketching the shape of a cage in front of me. I pictured thick bars in my mind's eye and made them of iron just for good measure. If Seelies didn't like iron, it stood to reason their creations would be susceptible to it, too. I slashed my hand horizontally to make sure they couldn't slip through the vertical slats.

They appeared to be circling me, keeping a wide berth as I worked. Getting them to charge me wouldn't be hard, but they were wise to what I was doing. I envisioned a door with a padlock, and it sprang into being. To my left, Avery had managed to undo the third and fourth locks. Only one more to go. I could keep these things occupied just a little longer.

A horrible thought popped into my head as I tried to discern how to get the monsters into my trap. It needed bait and they seemed awfully keen on me. They'd left Avery completely alone so far. Swallowing my fear, I backed myself toward the open cage door.

"Oi, uglies, come and get me you bastards!"

The trio of dog-lizard things snarled in unison

and raced toward me. I could feel Excalibur's pull to knock them down one by one. Somehow, I knew that would only make matters worse. The blows before had summoned the second, splitting the first in two. I didn't want any more of these things to show up.

"I need you to let this happen," I whispered to the blade.

It grew painful in my grip for a moment before subsiding, as if letting me know it hated the idea, but it wasn't going to stop me. Nice to know my semi-sentient weapon could take a hint. I was still too terrified to relinquish my grip on the sword in this place. I had just enough time to shift it back into bracelet form before the trio of creatures pounced, knocking me down. They were on top of me in seconds, their rows of sharp teeth gnashing at my throat, my arms, and any bit of me they could reach. I had just enough range of motion to summon the door to close and lock behind them. They were stuck now. But so was I.

That strange red mist began to cover every inch of me where the creatures touched. It wasn't painful, but it dulled my senses to the point I wasn't sure I'd have cared if they had been sinking literal teeth into my body. The darkness around me grew silent and held a calmness to it that called to me. Avery would get the last lock undone and get what we came for. That was the important thing.

For now, I could just lie here and let these things have me. As deaths went, this one would at least be memorable.

The mist swirled over my face, and everything vanished.

SEVENTEEN

Death wasn't supposed to hurt once it was over. So, why did it feel like I'd just been slapped across the face? I groaned, trying to bat away whatever had hit me. Wait, dead bodies weren't supposed to groan or have control of their limbs either.

"Get up, Morgan."

Nim's voice jolted me enough to open my eyes. The strange inky darkness I'd been in with Avery had been replaced by a more greyish color, tinged on the edges by a fine red mist. Just like those bloody dog-lizards.

"I'm dead, aren't I?"

Nim reached out and pinched my forearm.

"Ow!"

"Would you feel that if you were dead?" she countered.

"No." I rubbed my cheek again where I surmised, she'd slapped me to wake me up. "But you are."

She fixed me with a withering look. "Come now, Morgan, I taught you better than that. And besides, I would have thought your recent experiences told you that death doesn't mean we're gone for good."

My mind flashed to the Crystal Cave and my conversation with Ezri. She'd felt as real as me, just as Nim did now. I sat up, my body feeling sluggish. "Right. So, if I'm not dead, then where am I?"

Nim took in our surroundings. "Whatever those beasts were that you trapped, this is their doing."

"What?" I rubbed my head. "I don't follow."

"You thought you trapped them in your little cage. They're the ones who snared you, my dear."

"But how?"

"This is their domain. You entered without permission and your friend is seeking to tear down their defenses. What else would you expect a guard dog to do?"

"Not swallow me whole."

"You have not left that flat your friend owns."

"What, this is all in my head?"

"Oh, no it's really happening, but it's magic. An illusion."

"Seelies would know all about that ..." I muttered before catching a glimpse of the slender points of Nim's ears. "Sorry, not you."

She brushed a fingertip along her ear. "Ah, but I was quite masterful at it. I hid my true face from the world for nearly three decades."

"You were protecting me.

"And are these people not protecting what they hold most dear?"

"They let a man die. They used him and discarded him like he didn't matter."

"So, they are the enemy."

"Of course, they are." I managed to get on my feet and began pacing in a small circle. "Avery should have broken through the last lock by now."

Nim shrugged. "Time is strange in places like these, in the shallows made of magic. I suspect when you emerge, you will find little time has passed."

I couldn't decide whether that was a good or bad thing. I kept pacing, trying to sort through my thoughts. "This is a magical construct linked to a computer game." A phrase she'd used stuck out to me—*guard dog*. "You're right, they're treating us like a computer would treat a hacker. They're like ... antivirus software. Magical antivirus."

"I knew you would figure it out. You always were a clever girl."

"Not that I'm not thrilled to see you, by the way, but are you just going to lecture me?"

She smiled and it lit up her eyes. She pulled me in for a tight embrace and for a split second I let the grief of losing her come to the surface.

"No tears now," she whispered. "Time to be the brave hero you were born to be."

"Fighting them head on only made things worse. Every time Excalibur touched them more appeared."

"So, you've learned something."

"But I don't know how to fight them then. Trapping them didn't work."

"Your mistake was using yourself as bait."

"What else was there to use?"

"Illusion." Nim's voice came from behind me.

I whirled around to find another version of my aunt standing there. Her features were more blunted, closer to human. This was the woman I'd known all my life. The one who'd tended my scraped knees and filled my head with fantasies of a place far away, a kingdom that would one day be mine.

"You are destined to be a queen, Morgan. You

have immense power inside of you ... to do what most witches can only dream of," the illusionary Nim said.

"I don't know ..." I thought back to the tournament and how I had managed to use a bit of illusion then. But nothing like what I was facing here.

"Start small. Give them something else to chase," the more fae Nim said.

"Giving them something else to focus on sounds great, but how the hell am I supposed to do that from inside here?"

"Figure out what makes them uncomfortable. Use that to get out," both Nims answered at the same time.

What the fuck does that even mean?

They vanished from sight before I could get any more out of them. For a moment I stood in the grey space and shivered at the sense of loss hitting me all over again. Wait, maybe that was something. Computers didn't tend to do well if they overheated. Maybe these manifestations were heat adverse, too?

I rubbed my hands together like I was trying to light a fire and pictured flames emerging from my fingertips. A hint of lime filled the space as a tiny globe of greenish flame materialized along my skin. Just like the light I'd cast in the fog. I stretched my hands out as if I were pulling dough apart. The globe grew, elongating in my hands until it broke into several spheres. I lobbed them at my surroundings, and they continued to blaze when they made contact.

Sweat prickled along my neck instantly and I could almost smell something like burning plastic.

"Ahh!" Avery's voice filled my ears. She sounded startled and as the burning plastic smell intensified, I realized my magic hadn't been precise enough. It was doing damage to the systems she was trying to access.

I spread my fingers and held my arms out to my sides. I imagined the flames receding back into my body and they obeyed. Still, the space around me seemed to almost come alive. The mist at the periphery brightened and thickened.

So, fire was the wrong approach.

"Uh, Avery don't know if you can hear me, but I think I need to make things a bit chilly for a minute."

No response.

Well, there wasn't time to worry about her. I wasn't going to do anyone any good stuck in this weird cyber prison. I shifted my focus to bringing the temperature down. The air around me—or at least what resembled air—grew cold and my breath came out in plumes of cloudy fog. I shivered with every breath, but it seemed to do the trick.

The grey turned paler, almost a blinding white. With a strange sensation as if someone had shoved me from behind, I found myself lying on my back as the creatures skittered away from me. The bars of my cage were gone. Much like Nim had predicted, Avery was still working her way through the final lock.

Okay, time to keep these things occupied.

I wasn't entirely sure how to replicate myself. I know I'd seen Arthur do it, the Seelie prick, but I didn't understand the mechanics. At first, I tried to picture two of me and will the second version into existence, but my magic sputtered at the attempt. Still, it had to be possible.

'Let go and be free.'

Nim's voice played through my head like a voice on the wind. I'd never been very good at being free with my magic or letting go for that matter. But I was willing to give it a shot. I shook my arms out and let the tension ebb away.

I just needed to distract these things for a few minutes more. I let my power settle over me like a warm, comforting blanket. It reassured me that it was all going to be fine. I took a step backward and while that feeling remained, I could feel the lack of weight around me.

When I opened my eyes, a vibrant green after-image of me stood before me; almost like the golem I'd created during the tournament. I suppose those tricks were bound to come in handy again. She gave me a wink, turned, and darted off straight through the trio of dog-lizards. They yelped as she touched them and gave chase. I watched in awe as she darted from place to place, never giving them a chance to get their teeth into her.

"Got it!" Avery exclaimed and nearly broke my focus.

"Grand. But would you mind being quick about whatever it is you're about to do now? I can't keep this up for long."

"Just give me a minute. There are some files in here," she muttered and in an instant thick manila envelopes appeared in her hands. Fascinating.

"Let's get out of here," she said.

"Any idea how?"

"Release the magic?"

"You're the one who brought us here," I reminded her.

"Oh, right."

She looked at the documents in her hands and

her brow creased as she thought through some problem I couldn't begin to fathom. After a moment, she traced something in the air and shoved the files into it. They vanished into the darkness, and she looked relieved.

"I'm not going to ask what that was," I told her and reached for her hand.

"I'll explain later, when we're out of here."

She took hold of my left hand and the metal on my wrist warmed again. Behind us, the creatures howled, and I could feel my magic beginning to falter. It really was time to get the fuck out of here. But how? All I saw around us was the inky darkness we'd encountered on our arrival.

"We need a doorway," Avery said.

"I'm not seeing anything that looks like a door."

Avery's hand gripped my wrist. My hand jerked forward and for the first time, Excalibur shifted form of its own accord. The sword acted like a divining rod, guiding us from where Avery had done her work, away from the beasts still on the hunt until we came to a small red door with a blinking 'Exit' sign overhead.

"Thanks," I told the blade as it returned to my wrist.

"You really talk to it like it can respond?" Avery sounded equal parts skeptical and bemused.

"It's hard to explain," I said as we pushed the door open, and stepped through together.

Our hands drifted apart as the flat's living room came into view. Agent DeWitt, Fran, Jules, and Emerys all stood where we'd left them. Avery still sat on the couch. My eyes hurt from the light, and I pressed a hand to my head.

"Easy," Jules said, moving to support my weight.

"Did you accomplish what you needed?" Emerys' question came from directly to my right as she moved to aid me.

I heard movement on the couch, but still couldn't bring myself to open my eyes. Fingers tapped on keys and then Avery said, "I got it all."

I sighed and the ache in my head lessened enough for me to blink a time or two. The room slowly came back into focus. "What exactly did we get?"

Avery's cheeks turned bright and rosy at my question. "Everything possible, I mean, I didn't have time to read anything before we got out of there."

I nodded and waited as she focused back on the computer screen. Her face went pale, and I could see her hands shake in her lap.

"What is it?" Agent DeWitt crossed the distance in two long strides and was at the blonde woman's side.

"They knew about the pendant." The words were barely audible.

"But we already knew that," I said.

"I mean, they knew a lot more. Traced my family tree back to when the pendant was given as a gift. They have accounts of other people trying to steal it from my relatives. They knew everything."

"They also had to know you and your family had magic," Jules pointed out.

"So, why wait until now to try again?" I wondered aloud.

"I mean, I guess I'm vulnerable," Avery answered. "No family here in Boston. I live alone. Any protection Des and his bloodline could have given me is long gone with them."

"And if they've been studying you, then they must have figured out the defense mechanism on the pendant only lasts so long," I noted.

Avery looked over to Agent DeWitt. "Is this enough to do something? To bring charges?"

"We find the people who sent these messages, who planned this attack, and I will personally arrest their asses."

"Thank you."

Through all of this, Fran had remained silent. I turned my attention to her and found her sitting with eyes wide as coins and mouth slightly agape. She was clearly in shock at whatever Avery and I had done. Then again, from what I could tell, it didn't look like we'd done anything.

"You, okay?" I said, tapping the woman on the shoulder.

"Y-Yeah. This is all just a lot."

"You don't have to be involved anymore," I told her.

"Except I think I do." She glanced at Agent DeWitt. "They're going to need someone to corroborate what Leyton did and what they promised him. I can do that."

"I appreciate it," Agent DeWitt said. "And I'm sure Avery does, too."

"More importantly, I think Leyton would appreciate your support," Avery said, regaining her composure.

"So, we have proof they targeted Avery. But we're still no closer to finding them," I reminded the group.

Just then, Avery's computer gave a 'ping.' The screen which had displayed the online game faded, replaced by a large window announcing that the IP address had been triangulated. Could we really be about to confront these assholes and get back what they'd taken? Avery navigated through a couple of other screens to reveal a satellite view map of Boston. None of the geography made sense to me, but both she and Agent DeWitt seemed to recognize street names and surrounding locations.

"It's going to be complicated to get in now," Avery said.

"Now? You can't be serious," I protested. "It's the middle of the night. And that would definitely be considered breaking and entering."

"I'm all for a little light grey hat stuff, but even I agree that would stupid," Fran chimed in.

"Hitting them now is our best chance at keeping them off guard though," Avery insisted.

"Not to mention, the hackers holding Camelot hostage are about to unleash who knows what level of destruction in a day, if we don't get back in time," Jules reminded me.

"Okay, I get it. We strike now and we end it."

I just hoped we weren't walking into a trap.

EIGHTEEN

Despite being willing to stick around to give her testimony, it didn't take long to convince Fran that what we were about to attempt was not something she wanted to be party to. I had no doubt magic was about to take center stage and she had no way to defend herself.

"You sure this is going to work?" I asked, eyeing Agent DeWitt as we walked in a tight cluster toward a looming glass building labeled as the JFK Federal Building on the map Avery's phone displayed.

"Do I love the idea of having you impersonate federal agents to gain access afterhours to a commercial building downtown? No. Will security buy it? Only if you let me do the talking."

"Is your team going to be mad you aren't looping them in?" Avery asked.

Agent DeWitt gave a wry smirk. "You really think they don't know what's going on right now? The minute I called Duncan for that favor, he blabbed to the other two. Besides, Molly's been involved since the meet-up at the bar."

My head was still sore from the magical show-down with the dog-lizard antivirus creatures, and I couldn't keep any of the names straight as they talked. If I had enough brain power to link names to faces, great. But it wasn't like we were sticking around long enough for it to matter.

Agent DeWitt led us past a security desk, waving her badge at the man behind the monitor. He nodded mutely and we ascended in an elevator to an unremarkable floor with boring walls and squeaky floors. She tapped a different badge at an unmarked door, and it opened with a click to reveal a cluster of cubicles that all sat empty. Voices drifted out from a large conference room at the back, which appeared to be our destination.

"So, these are the people we've been sticking our necks out for all week?" a brunette woman who looked a few years younger than me said, appraising us.

"They come with high regards," Agent DeWitt said.

"Yeah, from who?"

"Ezri sent them."

The redhead's name garnered a moment, a silent appreciation amongst the assembled group before the brunette nodded. "Even after all this time, she's still looking out for us."

"She said I'd find allies here," I offered, diving into the conversation.

"She wasn't wrong there," a blonde woman with a short bob replied. She offered her hand for me to shake. "Agent Molly Cartwright and this is Agent Kayla Rogers."

"Morgan le Fey, uh ... technically Crown Princess to the kingdom of Camelot."

Agent Cartwright let out a low whistle. "Should we be bowing?"

"Please don't."

"Now that the pleasantries are over, we need to get what we came for and head out," Agent DeWitt said.

"Jackets, vests, and tactical gear are ready. We'll be half a block out in case you need backup." Agent Cartwright gestured to a pile of equipment sitting on the table.

"No offense, but I'm not sure you'd be able to help," Jules said.

Agent Rogers let out a laugh before half her body went invisible. "Trust me, we're more than enough help if you need it."

"Right, well then, let's go storm the ... office?"

I immediately disliked the weight of the bullet-proof vest. I wasn't sure why we even needed them, seeing as our would-be attackers were most definitely magical. They wouldn't be shooting at us.

"You need to look the part. Now stop fidgeting," Agent DeWitt chided, batting my hand away from the strap around my torso.

"It just feels like overkill," I protested, but clasped my hands in my lap.

"Now, do you know what you're looking for once we get inside?"

"Not really. I was sort of hoping magic would sort of point the way."

"That trick your sword did certainly came in handy," Avery said from the backseat wedged between Emerys and Jules.

"Well, whatever you use to guide you, just be careful. These guys have clearly been calculated up to this point."

She didn't need to tell me that. It was obvious

this had taken a lot of planning. And if Avery was right, the enemy had chosen now to strike because her own magical defenses would have been lowered. It also meant they knew more than just who she was and the people in her life. And if they were as tech savvy as they appeared to be, there was no telling what our little incursion had tipped them off to.

The car stopped a block away from a nondescript multi-story building with darkened glass windows. Agent DeWitt shut off the engine and climbed out from behind the driver's seat. I hurried to keep up with her. "You really think this is going to work?" I questioned again.

"I think you might need the hospital trick," I heard Agent Cartwright call from behind us as she and Agent Rogers approached.

"The what?" Jules and I asked in unison.

"I can get you into the building unseen by cameras," Agent Rogers explained. "I'm a Whisperer." She let the word sink in before adding, "It might take a trip or two, but I can do it."

"Then what's the point of us being in these get-ups if we can just sneak in?"

"Plausible deniability," she answered in a cheerful tone. "Plus, I did a little digging on the way over and they don't have anyone at the front desk overnight. So, no one to see you coming anyway."

"Fine. Let's see what it looks like inside."

Agent Rogers stepped up and linked arms with Agent DeWitt and me. All three of us started walking towards a blank stretch of wall. Right before we would have collided with it, I felt her magic wrap around us like a protective bubble. Something about it soothed my nerves and I knew somehow that we were going to be just fine. Even the fleeting fear of getting half-stuck in a wall vanished a second after it occurred to me. Between one breath and the next we stood inside a back hallway that was dimly lit overhead with a pale orange bulb.

"Be right back."

Agent Rogers vanished from the hallway, so Agent DeWitt and I stepped back to give her room to bring Jules, Avery, and Emerys. They appeared a moment later before Agent Rogers vanished again. Avery looked around the space and back at her phone. She tapped the screen a time or two.

"It looks like it came from the fourth floor. I can't be sure exactly where until we're closer."

I peered around, spotting a door marked 'Stairs' at the far end of the hall. "Then I guess we go up."

I led the charge as our group of five ascended the

steps. Our feet echoed on each tread, and I regretted not casting a spell to muffle our approach. Too late now though. My nerves jangled as we arrived at the door that would take us onto the fourth floor. The beer from earlier was also starting to have more of an effect, dulling my senses slightly.

Agent DeWitt moved to the head of the group and crept into the space, weapon drawn, but held loosely at her side. She beckoned us onward, and we left the stairwell behind. There were only three large offices on the floor, each with their own sign. None of them conveniently read 'Evil Seelie Masterminds,' since that would have been too easy. Agent DeWitt tapped an earpiece protruding from her right ear.

"Molly, I need you to run a couple of names for me," she began reading off the names on the signs with tiny arrows pointing in different directions. "McPherson & Wayne, The Wilsher Group, and SFI Holdings."

We waited in silence for Agent Cartwright to pass along the information she found and for Agent DeWitt to relay it to us. She gave a head nod and pivoted to face us.

"The first is a law firm, does family and elder law."

"The second?" Emerys pressed.

"It's a property management company."

Neither option sounded like what we were looking for, but that left SFI Holdings by simple process of elimination. Something about the name sounded familiar somehow, but I couldn't quite place it.

"And the last one is a shell company for a larger tech conglomerate," Agent DeWitt said when I was already halfway to the door to the office.

"That sounds like what we're looking for," Jules concurred.

I reached the door and held my breath. The expectation of something about to happen was palpable, making my palms sweat as I reached for the door. Agent DeWitt swooped in, catching my wrist before my flesh made contact with the metal of the handle.

"The point is to leave as little DNA behind as possible." She pressed a blue latex glove into my hand.

"Sorry."

I tugged it on, the sweat on my palms managing to make it harder to don the glove. Once I'd secured it, I tried the door handle to find it unlocked. That sent shivers of unease down my spine. Part of me wanted to turn back and try again later. But my people were counting on me.

"What is it?" Emerys stood at my side.

"This feels too easy. It's nearly midnight on a weeknight. Everything else is locked up tight. Why would this place be wide open unless they were expecting us to pop by for a visit?"

Emerys held up her hands and I could feel power radiating from them. "Then we fight whatever they throw at us."

Taking a deep breath, I pushed the door inward and led the march into the unknown.

THE FRONT OFFICE WAS SPARTAN, but even in the night gloom, it shone. It was as if they'd used fluorescent paint on the walls and ceiling. The carpet was equally pristine and white. I almost felt bad treading on it. I didn't set foot a pace or two into the space before my left arm felt like it was on fire and the sapphire at the center of the bracelet blazed as if lit from within.

"I get it, you want to come out and play," I said, pressing my index finger to the jewel.

The heat receded as the blade transformed. It

had fast become a comfortable and familiar weight in my hands. I couldn't lie that I felt just a little more confident in having the sword at the ready. Taron would be pleased. The thought of him brought a smile to my lips. My companions fanned out behind me as we took in the surroundings. There wasn't even a desk where a receptionist could sit, nor were places available for prospective visitors to wait to be seen. This was absolutely a front. A single door with a frosted pane of glass led out of the lobby area.

"Looks like the only way forward is through," Avery said, taking a step so she was shoulder to shoulder with me.

"You ready to take back what's yours?"

"As I'll ever be."

With my still-gloved hand, I reached for the more ornate silver doorknob. Only this door was locked. I jiggled the handle; my pulse began to race and throb in my neck as panic started to set in. After a moment, something in the knob beneath my fingers shifted and poked me through the glove's barrier.

"Ow!"

I pulled my hand away and saw a spot of blood marring the otherwise pristine metallic surface. It appeared to glow before the barb disappeared and I heard an audible click from within.

I exchanged a nervous look with Avery before I tried the knob again. This time the handle turned, and the door swung inward on silent hinges. I couldn't quite explain it, but the air on the other side of the doorway felt almost familiar somehow. It made no sense in my head, and I had no rational explanation for what made me think it either, but I couldn't shake the sensation. I walked in, Excalibur held at my side and waited for the rest of the group to join me. Avery stepped in from behind, followed by Emerys.

"Maybe we should stay out here, just to be safe?" Jules called.

"My gut says we're going to need all the help we can get," I called back to her.

I didn't see Jules nod, but I heard her footfalls as she stepped onto the harder flooring beyond the frosted glass doorway. This space was darker than the lobby area and I fought the urge to reach for a light switch. I could hear something that sounded like fans running off to my left and I thought I caught snatches of a conversation. Then again, it could have just been my imagination playing tricks on me, feeding my desire to find what we came for and get the hell out of this place.

"What the hell?" Agent DeWitt's voice drew my attention.

I spun to see her standing in the doorway unable to pass over the threshold. I went to her and grabbed her by the wrist. I tugged as hard as I could, but she wouldn't budge. Even with Emerys taking her other wrist, we couldn't get her past the threshold.

"I'm afraid your friend isn't invited. It is a rather exclusive guest list after all," a baritone voice called from behind me. "Given what we do here, I'm sure you understand we can't be too careful who we let in."

I relinquished my grip on the agent's hands and turned back to find a tall man standing opposite me. He wore a simple V-neck shirt and dark grey trousers. I could almost say he was handsome except for the air of superiority wafting from him like overpriced cologne. As I studied the man's features, I was back in Leyton's memory. This was the bastard who'd taken the pendant from Leyton and left him to die.

"So, you are the foolish girl, coming to try and

stop our work. It's almost a pity I'm going to have to kill you."

"You've got something that belongs to a friend of mine. She'll have it back now."

He patted his chest and something bulky bumped against his fingers. He looped a finger through a delicate silver chain and produced Avery's pendant. "Oh, I think you'll find it has a new affinity."

I raised Excalibur, positioning myself to take a running leap at him with Avery, Jules, and Emerys behind me. If I was lucky the blade would land in his face.

He laughed, his elongated canines made him look almost vampiric. "Oh, you are welcome to try. In fact, I do hope you will indulge me."

He waved a hand and the frosted glass door slammed behind us. I could hear Agent DeWitt banging on the frame to no avail. Still, I wasn't alone in this fight. I felt Avery, Jules and Emerys summon their magic as the man surveyed us.

"This ends now," I yelled and lunged.

CHAPTER

NINETEEN

I wasn't prepared to slam into an invisible barrier. It knocked the air from my lungs, and I could feel Excalibur peel out of my hand. More than the lack of oxygen, my brain focused on the loss of the one thing that was meant to be mine and never desert me. I flew backwards, slamming hard against a wall.

"Morgan!" Avery's cry filled my ears and I saw her out of the corner of my eye as my vision started to blur and go black with spots.

"I told you, girl, that the pendant's allegiance has shifted. You cannot harm me," the man taunted.

I felt hands grab me by the biceps and hoist me on to my feet. Emerys pressed Excalibur's hilt back into my hand. "Try not to lose this again."

253

"Wasn't planning on it to begin with," I grumbled and straightened, taking stock of the man standing on the other side of the room.

My sudden movement must have triggered some motion sensor-based lighting, because the space suddenly flooded with overhead LEDs. In the harsh artificial lighting, the man looked even paler than I'd guessed before. His hair was thick and hung to his shoulders. His eyes—an earthy grass green—stared back at me, challenging me to test the truth of his words again.

But I wasn't that stupid.

We needed a different plan of attack. I looked at Avery. "Do you think you could … I don't know summon it or something?"

Avery's cheeks flushed at the suggestion, but she held out a hand and her fingers twitched. The pendant around the man's neck fluttered against his breastbone, but it didn't move. He shook his head and waved a hand in our direction.

Avery went sailing into the opposite wall, her glasses falling off in the process. "Pathetic," he spat and moved to lean over her, careful to remain just beyond reach. "You figured it out, didn't you? We have been watching you for some time."

"You must have been really bored then," Avery

quipped through gritted teeth as she struggled to sit up. The collision with the wall had knocked her off balance and she slumped back down onto her elbow.

"Oh, quite the contrary. For a little witch, you were quite intriguing. The little techno-mage, decrypting spells to help the police. I almost considered sparing you and enticing you to our cause." He shrugged a shoulder dismissing his own thought. The motion shifted his hair just enough to reveal a glimpse of his ear. It didn't look pointed, but Seelies were damn good at hiding their true nature. "Yes, you helped the police with their problems, especially the one, who thought she was so special ... well I suppose she wasn't that special if she's dead."

Heat and fury flooded my chest at the way he spoke about Ezri. I hadn't known her in life, and I'd only gotten a glimpse of her in death, but she was my blood, and no one talked about my family like they didn't matter. Emerys pivoted beside me, and I could swear she looked about ready to catch fire. Her hair was a vivid corona of red as energy coalesced around her.

"How dare you speak of my kin in such a manner," she snapped, hurling a swirling ball of energy at a spot just over his right shoulder.

He laughed, a horrible tinny sound as he focused his attention on her. "Oh, I suppose I should have seen the resemblance."

"Did your amateur spying tell you that Avery is one of the bravest people I've ever met?" I probed, hoping to draw his attention my way. I wasn't certain what Emerys was planning, but I knew she had far more skill than she'd just displayed.

"Witches rarely impress me," he said with a dismissive shrug. "Her skills are adequate at best."

"No, you called her intriguing just now. There's got to be something you saw that caught your eye." I gestured to the chain around his neck. "And I don't mean the pretty pendant."

"I misspoke," he corrected, taking a few steps away from Avery and back to the center of the room. "Not so much intriguing as confounding. She always seemed content to stay in the background, never taking praise that any other would have deemed their own to have."

"That's not what I care about. I care about helping people," Avery said, finally managing to get back on her feet. "I never did it for praise. I did it because it was the right thing to do. Even when it was hard, and it hurt. That's what good people do."

"Cling to your morality then, little witch. It is all

you'll have as you die," he declared and his finger-nails grew long, extending into talons.

Just like I'd seen in Leyton's fragmented memories.

In all the banter, I'd lost track of Julayne. I spotted her now behind the man. She crouched behind a low desk, her head brushing the bottom of a backlit sign featuring something that looked like fire and claws, not unlike what the man now sported.

"Is this your plan then? Are you going to talk us to death?" I taunted.

"Hardly," he scoffed, and the claws shot out a familiar red mist. I dove to the side before it could touch me. It splattered against the wall where I'd stood and appeared to almost eat through the paneling. I shuddered at the thought it could have been doing that to my flesh while we were stuck inside the computer program.

We needed a way to coordinate our efforts without letting him know what we were doing. If we'd had more time together to prepare, to practice, maybe we could have come up with a signal, or something to communicate our next move. We'd been so focused on just tracking down the pendant that this scenario had never occurred to us.

I stood, reaching out towards Emerys and Jules. They were the ones I held a closer bond with and the ones I trusted to be receptive to what I was about to do. For her part, Avery was lobbing globes of magic at the man. They bounced off him, the pendant doing what it was meant to do, even if it was corrupted by his dark power.

My magic snapped to the ready, eager as I started to tune the pair of them out. I focused all of my attention on the two women who'd walked through a portal with me less than a week ago, ready to follow my lead.

'I don't know if this is going to work, but we need to take him on together. He can deflect us one at a time, but we need to distract him.'

I put my intent out in the world, urging the magic around me to carry my message to them.

Jules stood and I could see the look of surprise in her eyes. I heard Emerys sigh on the other side of the room.

'This is new. I like it,' Jules' voice echoed in my head.

'We should bind him, so that Avery can reclaim the pendant,' Emerys added.

'That sounds great and all, but everything we try he just deflects,' I noted.

'We don't use magic. Not at first,' Jules suggested. Across the room I watched her mime tackling.

'It wouldn't work for long,' I reminded her.

'It wouldn't need to. So long as you can sever the connection between him and the pendant,' Emerys agreed.

I'd have to worry about how to do that once we got to that point. I gave them both a nod and Jules let out a guttural yell as she leapt out from behind the desk and launched herself onto the man's back. Emerys raced forward, trying to secure his wrists. They both struggled to hold tight as I moved to get between them.

I made a grab for the pendant hanging around his neck, but it was like my hand purposely missed. Of course, the defense mechanism. If I forced it off of him, I'd end up in no better condition than Leyton so long as the pendant bore this creep an allegiance. Besides, the flesh-eating mist coming from his claws was a deterrent to getting too close. But there had to be a way to get the pendant back to protecting its true owner.

'Blood may always be the strongest part of magic.'

Nim's voice filled my head, and it took all of my resolve not to turn around, hoping she'd be standing there watching over me. In that moment I understood what I needed to do. I just hoped Avery would forgive me.

I shoved Emerys aside, giving me access to Avery. I raised Excalibur and her eyes widened in fear. I mouthed the word 'sorry' before I raised the blade and brought it down across her forearm. The tiny red droplets flew into the air, and I could feel Emerys' power guiding them, as if she'd heard Nim's words, too. The blood droplets landed on the amethyst at the heart of the pendant, and they bubbled and sparked. The man looked down and his eyes went wide in disgust.

"How dare you!"

Avery pressed her hand to the small cut on her arm. I thought she was trying to staunch the bleeding, but a moment later, the red liquid coalesced into a thin string, as if connecting itself to her. It lashed out like a whip and curled around the pendant. Everywhere the blood made contact, the pendant glowed a vibrant pink hue.

He bucked and Jules went tumbling off his back. She landed on her feet and teetered for a moment before securing her balance. Beside me, Emerys' hands moved in a graceful dance and bright flashes of light popped into existence as she anchored bits of a spell to different points in the room. Jules seemed to catch on, and she bent low, drawing the flooring up so it kept his feet immobile.

Avery kept feeding the pendant her blood until the whole thing—gold casing and all—had turned pink. It thrummed and when it settled back against the man's chest jewelry ate a hole right through the fabric of his shirt. His talons did their best to break the contact before it could touch bare flesh, but they turned out to be the wrong implement for the job.

I could save him the trouble. Shifting Excalibur to my right hand, I lifted the blade in an upward jabbing motion, severing the amethyst from the thin chain. The pendant launched into the air and as if drawn by magnetism, it landed in Avery's bloody hand. I watched in stunned silence as the wound on her arm healed and the rest of the blood coating her palm vanished, as if it had never been spilled.

"I think you will find that the pendant has been reunited with its true owner," Emerys said as her bright spells wound around the man's wrists and torso.

I took a step closer and instantly regretted it. The pendant had left a blistering wound that oozed from his chest and stank of rotting flesh and bile. It turned my stomach, and I took a step back just to keep from being sick.

"You think you have won, but this is merely one piece in a much larger game," he wheezed.

"Tell us how to reverse the hack and regain control of my kingdom's systems ... and maybe I can get you some medical attention for that wound," I said.

He laughed and it was less bitter this time, raspier. "You assume I know what you are talking about."

"I was sent here to find that pendant. The two things aren't mutually exclusive. So, tell me how to save my kingdom."

"The princess who makes threats. Now that is fascinating."

"You don't know a thing about me."

"The stolen heir, finally come home to her true land. I only know what I need to ..."

"He's not going to give us what we need. Let's just leave him," Jules said.

I had half a mind to leave him here. Except this bastard needed to pay for what he'd done to Avery and Leyton, which meant that Agent DeWitt and her team needed access to both him and his technology. I looked around the room, spotting glowing sigils in the corners. If I had to guess, they kept anyone without magic in their blood from entering. Time to get rid of those.

I smiled a little as I turned one hand palm down toward the carpet and pushed myself off the floor and up to the ceiling. I slashed at each of the sigils with Excalibur before returning to the floor. The door to the room opened and Agent DeWitt entered, weapon raised.

"Everyone okay in here?"

"The people who matter," Jules muttered.

"Did you get what you came for?"

"Part of it. We still don't know how we're supposed to save my kingdom," I answered.

As if acting of their own accord, the pendant and Excalibur started vibrating so violently that they both shot out of mine and Avery's hands. The man winced as the tip of the blade zeroed in on his left front pocket. The pendant hovered, as if acting as a beacon. In a blur, Excalibur moved in a swift downward motion and a small drive fell to the floor. I bent and picked it up, hurrying to put distance between us so his wound didn't touch me.

Something was written on it in faded ink, but I thought it could have spelled Camelot. I glanced at Agent DeWitt, and she gave me an approving nod. I pocketed the drive to take with us. I'm sure Avery could figure out what to do with it.

"For what it's worth, I hope you live a long time, so you can rot behind bars," Avery said, eyeing the man.

"Oh, don't you worry. We'll do everything we can to keep him alive," Agent DeWitt promised just as more footsteps echoed in the hall beyond the lobby. The rest of her team, including a man I hadn't seen before, but assumed he was Duncan, rushed in with weapons raised. They eased their urgency when they saw that the target was already detained.

"We are going to need you to let him go, so we can take him into custody." Agent Cartwright addressed me directly.

I gave the go ahead to Emerys and Jules, and in unison, they released their spells. The man fell to his knees only long enough for Agent Cartwright to swoop in, securing his hands in handcuffs. I didn't know if they made them with iron, but part of me hoped there was even just a little bit of it in there to irritate the fuck out of him.

"I don't know about anyone else, but I could use a nap," I announced once the agents had taken the man out of the space.

Avery looked around the room. with a glint in

her eye that signaled curiosity. "I'd love to know what else they're hiding here."

"It's late. You should at least try to get some rest before you head off for the next part of your journey. Whatever that is," Agent DeWitt said.

"Rest sounds like a great idea." I had just enough energy to make it back to the car at street level before I succumbed to fatigue and the world faded away.

TWENTY

Every part of me ached from the prior day's ordeal. Still, we'd come out the other end victorious. We'd reclaimed Avery's pendant and even secured the code that would free Camelot from the hacker's grip. And I couldn't deny having a certain sense of satisfaction seeing Emerys, Jules, and I together, our magic connecting us when we needed it most. Maybe that's what was meant to happen. As I built the supports around me, the magic would grow ever stronger.

"You look deep in thought," Emerys noted, appearing from the tiny kitchenette with a cup of coffee in hand.

"Just amazed that we managed to make it through," I answered.

"I truly believe you are presented these tests to prove you can rise to the challenge. I do not believe you will face anything you cannot overcome."

"I appreciate your vote of confidence, and if I weren't so bloody bone tired, I'd let that buoy me all the way home. But nothing I did here was solo."

"I did not say you were meant to walk this path alone. I would have thought that became obvious upon our first journey here to seek the chalice."

"I guess the whole Chosen One title feels like it's supposed to be a solo act."

"You were chosen, because you have the power in your blood Morgan. You will learn in time how to shape that power to inspire others. You did it here and now with Avery. And with her mundane friends, she is leaving behind."

Avery had left her flat early to meet with Agent DeWitt, J.T., and a few other people whose names I'd heard tossed around a time or two, but had little frame of reference to remember them. I hadn't intended to ask her to uproot her entire life to save Camelot. Part of me had hoped with the code we'd taken from the game designer, we'd be able to go back through the barrier and our people could sort out how to use it to regain control of the network.

But Avery had insisted that her place was in Camelot. I wasn't going to argue with her.

Jules emerged from the bathroom looking refreshed, her hair slicked back in a knot at the nape of her neck. She looked almost relieved to be leaving this world behind. Maybe she was starting to see Camelot as home, too.

"So, should we be looking at flights back to London?" She slipped past Emerys into the kitchen and grabbed some coffee herself.

As much as I could use the sleep—as disjointed as it was likely to be—we were woefully short on time to return to Camelot before the hackers' deadline. "I'm going to portal us back to Ireland."

"That sounds like a big job." Avery's voice came from the doorway, and I turned to look at her.

Her face showed no evidence that she'd been crying, but I could sense the sadness that surrounded her. It was never easy leaving what was familiar. "Yeah, well, I don't think we've got much choice."

"You came here via a plane though. If you ever need to travel again, it will look suspicious you don't have return stamps."

"We can address those discrepancies upon our return to Albion," Emerys said.

Avery gave her a quizzical look, but dropped the subject. "Well, I'm ready to go whenever you all are."

"I can probably keep a portal open long enough for myself and one other person to get through, but not everyone," I admitted.

Emerys gave me a solemn look. "You do not need to do this alone."

"You're sure you can handle it?"

Her solemn expression turned to one of irritation. "Have you forgotten who taught you to create portals?"

"All right, I didn't mean to insult you."

"You two go on ahead. I need to grab one last thing," Avery said to Emerys, darting into the bedroom.

Emerys pressed a hand to the necklace she always wore and traced a circle in the space in front of her. The sweet air of Ireland filled the flat and I could see the slope of the hill that would take us down out of sight through the gate back to Albion. It was impressed that she could get that close. I just had to hope we wouldn't be spotted by any nosy tourists. I could see the strain in her expression as she held the spell open. Jumping whole continents was still a bit much.

"Right, Julayne, go on through."

"We will be waiting on the other side," Emerys said, resting her forehead against mine for a moment before stepping through the portal and vanishing from sight.

Out of the corner of my eye, I saw Avery lay her wedding band on the table.

"It seems silly, but I feel like I need to keep this promise to Des ... that one day I'll come home."

"No judgment here."

She settled the pendant against her chest, letting the stone gleam in the early morning light as she stepped up beside me, a small suitcase in one hand and a laptop bag slung over her shoulder. "Let's go save your kingdom."

Straightening, I raised my hands. For the briefest of moments, my magic fought my desire. It was almost like I'd slipped back in time to four months ago, before Nim's death and all of this started. But I pushed the doubt from my mind and concentrated, picturing the portal opening in front of me. I sketched a circle again and just as before the slope of the ground in Ireland appeared.

"So, I just walk through?"

"Yep."

Avery hoisted her case to hip height and stepped through, leaving me standing alone in her flat. I glanced at the ring sitting on the table. "Thank you for letting me have her, even if it's just for a little while."

I stepped through and the portal snapped shut as soon as my feet hit the grass. I heaved a sigh of relief when I wasn't overtaken with the urge to be sick. Avery stood beside me looking around, taking in the scenery while Emerys and Jules already stood at the foot of the incline.

"This is beautiful," Avery noted as we started down the hill toward the others.

"Trust me, it's got nothing on Camelot."

The four of us walked on and as if it had become the norm, the world subtly shifted around us until the open fields were replaced by thick branches and brambles. Emerys reached out a hand and Avery's case began levitating beside her, avoiding the snarls of the underbrush. We walked past the mouth of the Crystal Cave, and I could almost hear Ezri's voice calling out to me, telling me I'd done well. Even if it was my imagination, it brought a smile to my lips.

I hurried on as we cleared the forest and the sprawling lake before us. I scanned the sky in the hopes of glimpsing a certain dragon only finding nothing but clouds. On autopilot, my feet carried me the rest of the way to Emerys' cabin.

I didn't have a chance to open the door before it swung inward on its hinges and my friend appeared, throwing himself at me. "Thank God you're home." His glasses sat askew on his nose when he pulled back to look at me.

"Not that I don't love the enthusiastic greeting, mate, but it does seem a bit disproportionate given the circumstances. Also, last I saw, Emerys had portaled you back to the castle."

"I was miserable without you all. Her Majesty noticed and sent me here. She figured you'd have to come back this way." I picked up a hint of embarrassment as he spoke about my mother. "She said she didn't trust anyone else to be here when you returned."

"Have things shifted for the worse?" Emerys asked from behind me.

"Funny you should say that," Gethin said.

The floorboards creaked as someone stepped down the stairs. Breath caught in my throat for a moment until the shadow within resolved into Taron.

"What are you doing here?" I demanded, resisting the urge to give him a similar greeting to the one Gethin had shown me.

"Your communications may be hampered, but

ours are not. And it became clear very quickly that you had left. I wasn't going to let you simply come back without making certain you were all right." Had he and my mother been in cahoots then?

"He showed up three days ago and wouldn't leave," Gethin grumbled.

Avery moved to whisper in my ear. "I'm guessing he's the dragon?" She made a quick gesture towards Taron.

I nodded wordlessly. It took a moment to find my voice again. "I appreciate you being concerned about me, but as you mentioned, Camelot's got some serious communication issues. And we've got a way to fix them."

"If we can get back to the palace in time," Jules reminded me.

"Can't you just portal us?" Gethin looked hopeful.

"I could always take you," Taron offered.

"I don't know if I can manage another portal right now," I admitted and turned to Emerys. "What about you?"

She took a deep breath. "I suspect I could handle the trip for the rest of us."

"Remember, we are on a timetable," Jules said,

giving me a wink that did nothing to hide what she thought lay in my immediate future.

"Oh, sod off"!" I said playfully.

I watched as Emerys led the rest of our company a short distance from the cabin before ushering them through a portal she manifested. It was better that she get Avery to the castle now anyway. I didn't need to be there for the techno-magic. At least I hoped not. When I turned back, Taron had already disrobed.

"You really just came to annoy Gethin for three days, because you were worried, I wouldn't come back?"

He shrugged one bare shoulder. "I may have also made a wager with Talia as to when you would return. She thought you would arrive too late, and we'd find ourselves in the throes of battle."

"Well, I appreciate you had the better odds."

"You know, one of these days I would like to join you on one of these adventures," he said.

"That would not be a good idea. Not if we wanted to get anything useful done." I made a circular motion. "Come on, can we hurry it along a bit?"

He let out a laugh. A moment later, a dragon sat

where the man had been. I nestled myself in his front legs and held tight as he took to the sky. I shivered as the air temperature dropped the higher, we rose. Taron held me tighter and blew out puffs of smoke, his chest warming with the effort. Before long, the sight of Camelot's castle came into view, and he landed outside the courtyard. He eased me to my feet and shifted back.

"Shit, your clothes," I hissed.

"Not the first time we've caught him skulking naked," Shunae's voice called from around the corner. She appeared with a pair of trousers and a shirt.

Taron offered her a bow and accepted them. "Much obliged."

"You're lucky I like you, Your Highness."

Maybe my assumption a week ago that being seen arriving here by dragon would be scandalous was an overreaction. I filed it away for later reflection. "Did everyone else get back?" I hurried to fall into step with the other woman.

"Yes, your new friend is in with the Queen and the Council now. But you ought to be there, too. They've got questions."

I took off at a sprint, bursting through the front doors much to the annoyance of the guards standing watch. I didn't look back to see if the others were following me. My time in this place might have been brief, but muscle memory is a wonderful thing and my legs carried me to the Council Chamber. Avery stood over a laptop holding the drive we'd taken from the hackers in Boston.

"You are unharmed," my mother said.

"Had a few scrapes along the way, but we can end this before anyone gets hurt," I said. "It turns out these ... hackers were operating on the other side of the barrier, too."

"Let's hope this works," Avery said and slid the USB drive into the computer. I moved to stand behind her and watched as the screen shifted from the red countdown to one that listed a series of options, including the command 'Cancel Count-down.' Avery tapped the down arrow key three times and selected it. The pendant around her neck grew vibrant, as if she stood directly in a sunbeam and I could feel power emanating from it.

"What's going on?" my mother asked.

"I ... I think she's granting us its protection," I said.

"The gem at the heart of the pendant pulsed three times as she hit the key to end the strangle-hold on our systems. A wave of energy swept out from where Avery stood, cascading outwards. In an instant the systems came back online and everyone in the room breathed a collective sigh that this crisis had been averted.

"Your Majesty, we should get you in front of the cameras denouncing what occurred and to reassure the people that all is well," one of the advisors said.

"And to make it clear to the Seelie bastards they aren't getting their prisoners back," I added.

Taron, who'd been standing just out of view, stepped forward with a confused look on his face. "This was not Seelie magic."

"Of course it was. They demanded the release of Seelie prisoners. They threatened to start a fucking war," I argued.

"You would have no way of confirming it, but we were on the outside. The Seelies were cut off just as Camelot had been." Taron didn't seem bothered by my anger or the fact I had pushed back against him.

"You are certain?" My mother addressed him.

"We are not friends with Uther and his ilk, but that doesn't mean we don't have ways of keeping tabs on them. Their defenses and systems were crippled nearly the moment yours were."

"So, if it wasn't the Seelies then who was it?" I blurted.

"A good question. One I think is in all of our best interests to resolve," Taron replied.

"Uh, not to interrupt what is clearly a very important political debate, but something's happening," Avery interjected, drawing focus back to the computer on the table in front of her.

A symbol spun on the screen—like a screensaver, but more ominous—as if waiting for our next move. I'd seen it in the building where we'd recovered the drive and the pendant; a flame overlaid on what looked like a stylized eye. Beside me, Taron made an undignified noise.

"You know what this is."

He rubbed at his chin, clearly trying to convince himself whatever he thought he knew wasn't the truth. "I didn't think they existed anymore."

"Who?" Emerys' voice was sharp, probing.

"The Syndicate of the First Inferno."

Emerys appeared to recognize the name as well and her cheeks went pale. "Neither did I." She steadied herself against the table. "This changes things."

"Would someone tell me who the hell these bastards are?"

Taron looked at me, his expression having gone stony. "I'm afraid they're dragons."

Dragons.

———

A QUICK AUTHOR'S NOTE

WHEN I ORIGINALLY DECIDED THAT the Guardians of Camelot series would be set in the Seasons of Magic universe, I knew I wanted to have some crossovers happen. I'll be honest, I didn't quite envision quite so many happening as did in this book. But in the end, I quite liked how it really tied the series to the wider universe. And I felt it also helped establish the timeline more clearly. For those curious, this book is set very shortly after Agents of Magic book 3, *Untouched Magic.* It was so fun to see what these characters were up to and get the chance to view them from a whole different perspective. We know them from Kayla and Ezri's points of view, so it was fun getting to interact in a more formal way.

ONE OF THE things I really like about expanding this universe is getting to dig into characters we only scratched the surface of in other books, namely

Avery. I still find it amusing this character I hadn't intended to be that critical has evolved into the bridge across three series!

As I wrote the start of this book and Morgan and co. kept bumping into Ezri's inner circle, I did have moments where I was like "does everyone know this chick?" I thought it was appropriate for Morgan to have that reaction, too. It felt honest. In the end, though, I don't regret fitting so many people in. I also have great ideas for a little Morgan v. Jonathan "bartender-off". Fuel for a future short story for sure!

Now that we've firmly settled into the Seasons 'verse, I am looking forward to dipping back into Albion's lore more in the next couple of books. We barely scratched the surface of the Syndicate of the First Inferno, and they are going to play a much more prominent role in book 4, *Her Emerald Shield*. And I am stoked to have Morgan quest with some different companions, too! Things are about to heat up between her and Taron and I can't wait!

· · ·

Turn *the page for a glimpse at what awaits in Her Emerald Shield...*

<u>**HER EMERALD SHIELD**</u>

How deep does trust go?

Morgan's quest for the amethyst pendant may have brought her kingdom back from the brink of war, but the threat to her people remains. Uncovering the true culprits behind the cyber attack leads to more questions and uncomfortable truths about allies she isn't ready to accept.

Learning about Prince Taron's past forces Morgan to see the man in a new light. And when they discover a childhood friend is the ringleader of the hacking attempt, Taron pledges to aid Morgan in her next quest to make amends. Unwilling to let Morgan go unaccompanied, Gethin insists on joining the fight.

Morgan is eager for the time to truly get to know Taron as they pursue the escaped hacker. But even as they grow closer, his past threatens to drive a wedge between them. And as their journey takes them beyond the barrier and out of Albion, will Taron find Morgan's former world hostile? And can this quest guide Morgan to yet another knight to fill her ranks before they lose their quarry for good?

Scan the QR code to get your copy of Her Emerald Shield.

ABOUT THE AUTHOR

Sarah Biglow is a *USA Today* bestselling author. She lives in Massachusetts with her husband and son. She is a licensed attorney and spends her days combatting employment discrimination as an Investigator with the Massachusetts Commission Against Discrimination.

You can find an up-to-date list of all my books here